Acclaim for stories in this volume

Kinds of Kissing" is an admirably subtle tale of
nnocence and terrible secrecy, all told with fine

A. L. Kennedy

om a relatively new writer, "The Wall" is a remark-
red demonstration of what the short story can
a very few pages.'

Brian McCabe

writer whose work I've known and admired since I
across it in Polygon's *Original Prints*. Her stories are
ly crafted and provocative, revealing glimpses of the
areas of human nature.'

Janet Paisley

ry dip into life, justified by enchantment and the
Three Kinds of Kissing" smacks of innocence, and
kered advice for afficionados of embouchure, but it

Tom Adair

Superior Bedsits

and other stories

Helen Lamb

Polygon

© Helen Lamb, 2001

Polygon
An imprint of Edinburgh University Press Ltd
22 George Square, Edinburgh

Typeset in Galliard by
Hewer Text Ltd, Edinburgh, and
printed and bound in Great Britain by
Creative Print and Design, Ebbw Vale, Wales

A CIP Record for this book is
available from the British Library

ISBN 0 7486 6306 1 (paperback)

The Publisher acknowledges subsidy from

THE SCOTTISH ARTS COUNCIL

towards the publication of this volume.

For
Michael, Jennifer and Gareth

Contents

Acknowledgements

Some of the stories in this collection have been published in the following:

Three Kinds of Kissing (HarperCollins)
The Laughing Playmate (HarperCollins)
Original Prints (Polygon)
Meantime: looking forward to the millennium (Polygon)
Damage Land: an anthology of Gothic fiction (Polygon)
Marilynre várva: contemporary Scottish short stories in translation (Pannónnia Könyvek)
Chapman 83 & 94
NorthWords Magazine
West Coast Magazine
Scottish Child

'Three Kinds of Kissing' was broadcast on *Morning Edition*, RTE.

Helen Lamb

'Pointed Toes' was broadcast on *Morning Story*, BBC Radio 4.

'A Good Ear' was first broadcast on *Short Story*, BBC Radio 4, and subsequently on *Storyline*, BBC Radio Scotland.

'Long Grass, Moon City' was the winner of the Scotland on Sunday/Women 2000 short-story award.

Superior Bedsits

and other stories

Three Kinds of Kissing

I t's dark in here.

But not the kind of dark you get when you shut your eyes. That's not really dark at all. I can prove it. Here's something Olive taught me. You shut your eyes and screw them up tight until you see wee dots of light. Once you know how to do it, you can make them do things by squeezing your eyes different ways. You can make them shift and change colour. You can make the dots dance a polka or let them drift like balloons. Or you can take a tiny dot of light and make it grow until there's no darkness left.

Olive's my best friend. This is where we come when we don't want anybody butting in. She's not here yet. So I'm waiting. She got a bump on the head today.

This time it happened because she was clumsy and she spilled dish-water all over the floor. But it doesn't hurt much, she says. Only if she thinks about it. And she's glad it doesn't show because nobody – like me for instance – needs to feel

1

sorry for her. Olive gets bumps on the head all the time, but you don't notice because of her hair. She says its normal, but I don't know. Maybe it is.

She's taking her time. When I went to the door she wasn't ready and she said to come in but I didn't want to. You have to take off your shoes when you go into her house and my socks had a hole in one toe and weren't all that clean. So I said I would just wait here. She never has to worry about folk noticing the state of her socks and that kind of thing. Like being embarrassed to open the door because of the mess – I worry about that all the time. But her socks are always dazzling white and their house is perfect. Everything spit-new and spotless. They're always getting something else.

The latest thing is a nest of tables, three different sizes, made of glass. And nobody's allowed to use them. Olive says that's because they're occasional tables and you're not supposed to use them too often – just occasionally. She thought it was funny I didn't know that. She said I had a lot to learn and one other thing I should know is that it doesn't mean anything when her mum calls me love and kisses me the same as her.

According to Olive, there's three kinds of kissing. The first kind is just Ordinary Kissing. She wanted to call it pecking but I didn't like the way she said it down her nose like it was disgusting or something. Here are the rules for Ordinary Kissing:

An Ordinary Kiss lasts one second or less. You get it or give it but not both together. Usually, you get it on the cheek but you can get it other places as well. On the nose for instance. You only get it on the nose if they're in a good mood but you can get it on the cheek automatically. Automatic kisses don't have to mean anything, but we've noticed they nearly always mean goodbye. You get them when you go to bed and when you go out in the morning. Olive's mum kisses everybody automatically and it doesn't mean anything. She kisses Olive and forgets all about the bumps on her head. She kisses me too but that doesn't mean she likes me either, Olive says.

It's hot in here. I wanted to go swimming up at the dam today but Olive wasn't allowed because of the effluent being unhygienic. Effluent is germs, according to her mum, and she can't stand germs. She's very hygienic, she's always cleaning. Olive says she doesn't know when to stop. At night, in the bath, she scrubs Olive's knees with the nail brush and Vim and sometimes she scrubs so hard they're still red-raw in the morning.

She says her mum would put her in the washing machine too if she could get away with it. The whole bit. Pre-wash, hot wash, rinse and spin. Of course, she would be dead by the time she got to spin but she would be clean. Dead clean. Clean for ever and ever. She would never get dirty again. Olive said that would probably make her happy. She was laughing about it and birling round and round pretending she was in the drier, but she got mad when I asked about her socks. Would she wash her with them on or off?

The bump on Olive's head is like a wee blue bird's egg, but you can't see it because of her hair. I'm the only one that knows and I'm not supposed to tell anybody. She says if I do she'll send me to Coventry. Nobody speaks to people in Coventry, but Olive says they deserve it because they were not good friends.

She says she's my best friend and I can trust her, but she's not sure if she can trust me. Sometimes, she thinks I'm not a good friend because I never tell her anything. She says everybody's got a secret but the only one I can think of is about this place and she knows that already. She says there must be something else. Maybe something to do with my mum. Something she wouldn't want Olive or anyone else knowing. But I couldn't think of any secrets. I could make one up though, if she goes on about it again. If she keeps on saying my mum must be boring.

She should be here in a minute. Some people are afraid of the dark but not me. I like it. It's private. And if it gets lonely, I just talk into myself. Talking into yourself is like silent reading. Your lips are not supposed to move. Some people don't know how to do it. They whisper and put other people off. Snottery Sneddon can't do it. He sits beside me. He has a problem with his nose. The problem is he doesn't know how to blow it. He snorts instead. One time I tried to stop him by sticking his head inside his desk. But it wouldn't shut right because of his neck. It got in the road and I could still hear him.

We tried to imagine Seriously Kissing Snottery Sneddon but we couldn't. Serious is the second kind of kissing. Here are the rules:

A Serious Kiss lasts more than one second but less than ten. You can do it with your lips open or closed depending on how serious you are. It's supposed to mean I love you and you shouldn't do it unless it's true because it's serious. But with married people it can get automatic and we've noticed it usually means hello. They do it in the kitchen when they

4

get home from work and if they forget it creates a bad atmosphere. You can't Seriously Kiss a friend, but you can practise with a mirror or the back of your hand.

The dark in here's not the kind of dark you get at night. That is bluey-black and cold. When it comes down it surrounds you, but it stays outside of you because the moon and the stars keep it from touching you. But in here it's more brown than black, and there's nothing between you and the dark. It hugs itself around you so tight you think you're going to choke and the warm stuffy smell of it gets inside you. It gets up your nose and into your mouth and feels like fur stuck down your throat. It gets worse if you start thinking about it. Usually, I don't have the chance to think about it because Olive's here and I have to concentrate on what she's saying. Because she sounds funny when I can't see her face. Kind of snuffly and faraway.

We used to come here all the time. Olive used to bring her torch. But then this boy came nosing about and now we don't come so much any more and we don't bring the torch because there's this wee crack down near the bottom of the door. You wouldn't notice it unless you were looking. He might be looking though and he would know we were in here.

This boy has brown eyes, brown skin and hair nearly the same colour. Olive thinks he's good-looking, but I don't agree. He looks a bit weird if you ask me. His head's too big for a start. It doesn't fit the rest of him. If his head was any bigger he would look like a cartoon. He's got a skinny wee body and a great big head, and they don't go together. It's the same with his nose. It sticks out too much. If it stuck out any more, he

5

would look stupid and Olive wouldn't go all soft and gooey the minute she saw him. She'd go yuck instead.

He asked if he could come in and play. He should've asked Olive. She would've said yes. But he asked me and I said no, a boy would spoil it.

The third kind of kissing is Cowboy Kissing. You do it with your mouth open and it lasts up to ninety seconds or as long as you can hold your breath. It's never automatic. If you kiss back, it's called French Kissing.

But when you resist it's a Cowboy Kiss. It happens in Westerns all the time, mainly in saloon bars and stables. The woman gets insulted and the cowboy gets his face slapped. If it happens in the saloon, he also gets whiskey poured over his head. Then he shoves her away and strides off through the swing doors laughing sarcastically. The main problems with Cowboy Kissing are running out of breath and falling in love. If you fall in love, it's THE END. This is why you have to resist.

Olive says we should practise so we get it right when it comes to the real thing. She's getting really good at resisting, but she slaps too hard and then she wants to do it again. It stings even worse when she uses water for the whiskey, and I'm getting fed up with being the cowboy.

Olive says she's never going to stop resisting. She doesn't trust any kind of kissing. It never means what it's supposed to mean. But I don't think she would've resisted if that boy had come back and kissed her. I bet she would've taken it seriously.

Do you know what she said once? She said she only plays with me because she feels sorry for me. I'm not a good friend. I never have anything interesting to tell her and she's doing me a favour hanging around with me. Nobody else could be bothered.

I don't know why I bother keeping her secrets when she talks to me that way. Do you want to know how she got the bump on her head? She spilled dish-water all over the floor and her mum battered her head off the kitchen wall. That's how. Olive says it's normal. It happens all the time. People get hurt in places that don't show, and if I don't believe her I can go to Coventry.

She's coming now. I can see a bit of her leg through the crack in the door. She's whistling. She's always whistling but it never sounds like any tune I know.

Hello.

Now shut your eyes and screw them up tight and tell me what you can see. Use your imagination.

Looking for Joe

O n Monday, Sarah rode the bus into town, up on the top
deck right at the front, clutching the purse in her coat
pocket, her other hand fisted around her thumb. A nervous
habit. She held it all in – and scanned the human current on the
street below. Tight-lipped business men, the tight wee steps of
high-heeled office-girls. They held it in too.

But the girl half a block away, now she was unusual,
striding along with a great big smile on her face. Whatever
thought had set her off, she couldn't contain it. Her happiness
was spilling over.

And, for a moment, Sarah's grip on the purse loosened and
her pinched little face relaxed. She had on a beige raincoat and
a silk scarf with four scenes from Paris. She'd never been to
Paris herself. Never been anywhere really. Her brother Joe
brought it back from his first trip abroad. He said the French
knew how to live. They had it sussed over there.

Later, he would say the same about the Portuguese, the

Greeks, the Italians and their dolce vita. Joe never settled after Paris, but, while their father was alive, he showed up on the doorstep once in a while with a couple of bottles of cheap red wine and tried to tell her how to live.

Joe and his drunken worldly arrogance railed against her parochial shrug. Joe and his harangue. *Where have you been? Where have you ever been in your life? When are you going to get out of this hole?*

The upside-down Eiffel Tower pointed its arrow down her back to where she sat. Sarah always sat up front if she could. She liked to see what was going on, nosed her way into town.

That girl, for instance, what was she so pleased about? She was smiling, still smiling, with an unguarded radiance so mesmerising Sarah nearly smiled too, unaware of the man at the top of the stairs. He came forward and sat down next to her. A pair of feet went up against the window. And then a loud phlegmy cough.

Her grip tightened round the purse again, tried to squeeze some reassurance out of it. She didn't see why he had to sit there. They had the entire upper deck to themselves. He could've sat anywhere, but some folk had no consideration. They sprayed you with their germs and stuck their feet up in your face. Not very nice feet either. She eyed the chewed-up trainers. The sole on the left one was coming away from the upper and a bit of damp sock poked through the gap, like a tongue, as much to say – are you looking at me?

She turned and frowned through the window but not really taking it in anymore. The happy girl had disappeared and now she was almost afraid of what she might see down there. The shoe upset her, reminded her of things. Another Monday, another bus. Or maybe it was the same bus. They all looked the same. It could have been the very same bus and she was looking through *this* window, watching a man in a beat-up overcoat as he wove his slow unsteady path along the road. He was taking exaggerated care not to bump into anyone and succeeded in missing two pedestrians and a lamp-post before the traffic lights pulled him up short. His head came up. And she was looking at Joe, looking straight into her brother's blue eyes.

She could have let him go then and, in a day or two, she wouldn't have been so sure anymore. The eyes would've faded, greyed into an uncertain memory. She could have stayed on the bus.

This was when the clutching began – as she followed him to the square. She held her fear in, held it tight, her knuckles white and shining in the dark recesses of her coat pockets, her heart contracted to a tough wee claw. She'd watched from a distance while he made his halting perambulation of the benches. A cigarette. Some loose change. Most of them just shook their heads.

He did a full circuit and started again. It was weird but somehow she had known he would. She'd seen it coming all along.

He'd nodded as if he was expecting her. 'There you are,' he said. 'Did you get my card?'

She shook her head and Joe just shrugged. 'The Javanese know how to live.'

11

'No hurry. No hassle,' he explained. 'But, like everything over there, the mail is ruled by the laws of fate.' He smiled his rare and distant smile and gazed straight through her, focused on something way beyond Sarah.

'You'll get it,' he said. 'When the time is right, you'll get my message.'

Every Monday, she came back to the square looking for Joe. She brought him cigarettes and donuts from the City Bakeries. She gave him money. He didn't want to come home. No point, he said. There was nothing for him in this country and he'd be back on his travels any day.

Her bag slapped against her thigh as she started along the road, hitting the same spot every time, gradually chafing its way through her clothes – raincoat, skirt, flesh-tone pantihose. It began to ache but still she kept the bag where it was, a nagging reminder of everything she had to lose.

Usually, he was there before her, waiting by the bench next to the statue of the man on the horse. Always the same bench. He never sat down, never paced. He just stood, very patient and still as stone. It was eery. Sometimes, she got the feeling he'd been standing for ever.

And then one Monday, he wasn't there. Three weeks in a row, she came and sat alone on the bench. It was restful without him. She found she hardly missed him at all. The fourth week, he showed up again, raving about Monte Carlo. He told her life was a gamble and she should take her chance before it was too late.

'Where have you been?' he roared at her. 'Where have you

ever been in your life?' Last week when he didn't come, she fed the donuts to the birds.

Sarah put the bag down between her feet, instinctively tensing her calves against it as she glanced about. No sign of Joe yet. They all looked the same to the casual observer – like the buses – unless you were waiting for one in particular. They went by in the street and all you registered was a dosser.

The square was busier than it had been in a while. Encouraged by a watery sun, a handful of hardy souls lingered optimistically on the benches. Last time she was here, the statues had outnumbered the living and she had been the only one sitting, apart from the man on the horse. She'd no idea who he was, didn't particularly want to know either. She'd never cared for statues much. Cold, stiff things. The subjects long dead and buried. They gave her the creeps.

Maybe that was what got to her about Joe. The way he stood there like a statue. He seemed more dead than alive.

And, sometimes, she was afraid of the shared history hidden in the stony folds of her brother's ancient overcoat. She didn't want to examine it too closely.

Across the square, a teenage boy was doing the round of the benches. He didn't seem to be having much luck though. Maybe because he was young. That put people off. And you couldn't blame them because a lot of the young ones were at it these days. She'd heard that. A lot of so-called beggars were raking it in.

He was sixteen, maybe seventeen, reddish hair. She watched him dart to the next bench, his head thrust forward, shoulders hunching sharply through his thin blue jacket. He made them nervous – that was the trouble. He moved too fast.

Sarah took a few coins from her purse ready for when he got to her: 4 tens and 5 twos. She gave the money a generous jingle, held it out as he approached. He had nice hair, really beautiful hair for a boy, shoulder-length coppery waves which fell across his face when he stopped.

'Fifty pee,' the boy said flatly. One by one, he dropped the coins back in her lap.

'Fifty – fucking – pee.' He shook his head, glowered down at her through all his furiously glinting hair – as though she was to blame for putting him in this position.

'Sorry.' Sarah gathered up the coins.

'Sorry,' he repeated. 'Sorry? Nobody asked you to be sorry.' He began to pound his fist into his palm. Then grasped it. Held it still. His hands were level with her face, raw and mottled with the cold and tattooed above the knuckles in blotched blue ink – the letters – s c o t. His name maybe. There was more. But she couldn't make out the other hand.

'Ach – you're a waste of time.' He strode across to the next bench. 'What is it with you lot?' he demanded. 'Tell me what it is.'

A pair of adolescent girls huddled together with their heads down, nudging each other and arguing about something. The skinny one thrust a paper poke towards him and her pal went beetroot.

'I don't want sweeties. I don't want your rotten sweeties. Aw that sugar's bad for you. Do they no teach kids anything these days? Do you no teach them anything?' He turned and glared back at Sarah.

And then he was off, kicking his way through the pigeons and shouting fuck off, fuck you all, as they scattered. He was just a boy, not much older than the girls, a couple of years at the most. Their daft laughter chased after him across the square, but Sarah couldn't bear to watch. When she closed her eyes, his hands were there again, the missing letters stamped painfully clear – L A N D.

Another fifty pence would have made no difference. He wanted to shout at her, at them all. The name was SCOTLAND and his silence could not be bought.

The girls had their heads up now, Tweedledee and Tweedledum chewing gum, acting bored like they'd seen it all before. The skinny one managed to look bold with it. Her pal just looked vacant.

Last time she saw Joe, he was going on about Amsterdam and how it put this place to shame. He could be right for all she knew. Maybe Amsterdam girls had better things to do. She got the donuts out of her bag. No point in letting them go to waste and it didn't look like he was coming now. But imagination wouldn't get him too far. He'd be back.

The birds crowded round her feet, big ones shouldering the scrawny ones out of the way and on the bench a gang of pigeons scrabbled to get near her. When the food ran out, they'd be off. She knew that. She had no illusions about this sudden upsurge in her popularity. She wasn't sentimental. Not like Joe.

Amsterdam, Paris, Rome – it didn't matter where he went.

There would be a square and statues and rich pickings. But over here or over there, it was the fat bird that got fatter. She carried on distributing the crumbs until there was nothing left and her hand finally returned to her pocket and froze around the purse. It was all she had to hold on to these days. The only thing that made a difference between them.

The Shadow Man

I t was the sound that first drew her attention. The click-click-click. Something insistent about the rhythm. Something she couldn't ignore. The way it came in rapid bursts. Stopped. Then came up closer. Every pause a wee bit shorter than the one before and the clicking getting louder, echoing like stiletto footsteps in her wake.

It cut off abruptly when Rachel turned and, in the fading light, she could just make out the shadowy figure of a man hunched inside a parka jacket, his head bowed towards her, the face obscured by a curtain of straggly hair. He seemed to slow down when she looked at him.

She turned back and it started up again. Only this time, Rachel thought she could detect a human quality to the sound. A tongue sucked against the roof of a mouth. Sucked – then pulled in some mysterious, syncopated code. She wasn't sure what it meant, or if it was directed at her or not, but she was relieved when she got to the main road and lost him in the noise and hustle.

Her raincoat flickered as she wove her way through the rush-hour crowds. The coat was shiny PVC, a brilliant acid yellow. She bought it not long after she came up to college. It made her feel less invisible. Back home, everything you did was noticed. It was a drag a lot of the time. But nobody even looked at you here. She couldn't get used to that, and during her first few weeks in the city, the islolation had hit her hard. Outside of the college and the flat, it was almost as if she didn't exist. She was just one wee minnow in the big wide ocean. She could walk the streets for days on end and never see anyone she recognised.

So it was strange that she should come across him again. She spotted him on the underground a couple of days later. He was at the far end of the carriage on the same side as her and, from where she sat, she still couldn't make out his face, but she knew it was him all the same. She remembered the parka and the hair, long scruffy hair, tinged green now under the artificial lights.

And on the escalator she heard it again, fainter this time but still distinct – the click-click-click punctuating the space between the muffled roar of the traffic above and the whir of trains below. This time, she didn't turn round.

It was hard to say when she knew for sure. He followed her for days like a niggling doubt at the back of her mind that she couldn't quite shake or put into words. Out on the street, on the move, she never got a chance to get a good look at him. Vague impressions were all she had to go on, snatched glances as she half-turned to cross the road, catching his reflection coming up behind her in a car window. He didn't try to speak to her, but he stopped when she stopped, waited outside the shops and fell in behind when she came out. Always at a regular distance.

He didn't seem to want to get closer, but he wanted to be noticed.

He made sure of that.

And now he was there again, framed in the baker-shop window, the familiar parka jacket flapping in the wind, ducking his head as he peered in across the glass display shelf and the cakes and scones. Rachel faltered halfway through her order. There was something inhuman about his immunity to the weather. The way he stood inside the billowing jacket, as though it didn't belong to him, as though it had been blown around him by accident.

'Have you made up your mind?' the girl behind the counter asked. She looked pointedly past Rachel to the man who'd just come in behind her. Rachel ordered a pizza to take away.

'You'll have to wait,' the girl said sharply. 'Five minutes?'

'That's okay.' She wasn't in any hurry to get outside now. She glanced back at the window. He was still there, just standing in the rain, his outline blurred in the steamed-up glass.

The shop assistant and the other customer were acting very friendly. She seemed wrapped up in what he was saying, putting warm donuts in the bag one by one without taking her eyes off him, her cheeks pink from the heat of the oven.

The man rested an elbow on the counter and leaned towards her confidentially. He pointed to the donuts. 'Is this all I'm getting?'

The girl smirked. 'Did you want something else?' A wisp of

blonde hair escaped from her cap and fluttered provocatively over her eyes.

'I wouldn't say no,' the man said.

He gave a low suggestive laugh and the girl's rosy flush deepened. She blew the hair back from her face and shot Rachel a sidelong glance. 'I'll just check and see if your order's ready.'

Soon there would be no excuse to stay. She watched the girl place a sheet of greaseproof paper inside a polystyrene box. Now that the shop assistant was occupied, the man turned to her and winked. 'Cheer up,' he said.

Rachel forced a smile. She wouldn't have bothered normally. But he seemed okay. There was a kind of democratic generosity in the way he dished out the off-pat charm, first to the shop assistant, now to her. You couldn't take it too personally. And there was something warm in his brown eyes that made her want to confide in him.

As soon as she pointed towards the window, she began to regret it. But it was too late. She saw them both blink, their heads tilt as they curved away from her, but, even as they turned to look, the man in the parka was moving off, a dull green shape dissolving into the half-light and the rain. The girl's eyes narrowed and Rachel saw the suspicion flitting across her face – *another crazy customer*.

'He was just looking,' the man said smoothly. 'Just looking at the cakes, that's all.' He smiled at the girl behind the counter and she responded with a slight shake of the head. The two of them shared a look of agreement. *They had a strange one here*.

Rachel recognised the look. She began to feel strange. Maybe they were right. She shouldn't have said anything. Maybe he was just some guy standing in the rain looking at cakes. She still had some doubts about him herself. He got no closer. Nothing happened. And with each passing day, he seemed more insubstantial, a less and less convincing threat.

She paid for the pizza and left the shop hurriedly. There was no sign of him now but that didn't mean he wasn't there. He could be watching from a doorway, waiting for her to make a move. A lumbering double-decker bus drove too close to the kerb and sent up a spray of dirty brown water. Rachel cursed. The pizza box was splattered and sodden. She felt like chucking it away, but he might notice. He might make something of it. She shouldn't have pointed him out. That had been a slip. Better not to give him anything to go on. No reaction. No sign of recognition.

She didn't blame them for not believing her. Half the time she didn't believe in him either. All she knew was one of them was crazy.

But this click-click-clicking couldn't be in her head. She stopped at the lights and half-turned to check. He was back again. And suddenly she got this flash of recognition. He seemed so familiar he could almost be a part of herself. No that wasn't it. More like her shadow. A dark projection of her own image. A shadow man.

When the green man came on, she didn't move. She tugged her hood forward and waited, crossing at the last gasp so that he would have to jump the traffic or let her go. She'd played this trick on him before. She could make him do things. Dangerous things. It was like a game of follow-my-leader.

The raincoat flickered as she moved, a bright-yellow beacon

flashing along the rain-streaked, grey street. The coat made it easy for him to pick her out. Rachel had been aware of that for a while now. The coat wasn't as innocent as it looked. It was leading him on, asking for trouble and, one of these times, it was going to surprise him. It would lead him through a door and disappear.

Then, it would be his turn to be scared. As the door slammed shut behind him, he'd sense her presence in the dark, but he wouldn't be sure whether the soft, animal breathing belonged to her or if it was the echo of his own fear.

The weather was slowing down the traffic. Cars crawled blindly nose to tail, the beat of windscreen wipers sounding like so many thudding hearts. There was no magic door up ahead. But maybe there was another way. She didn't know why it hadn't occurred to her before.

Just to stop.

Just turn and face him.

'Hey, you. I want to talk to you.'

A woman with a red umbrella stopped in the path between them. She glanced up anxiously and Rachel muttered, 'Not you. It's okay.'

The woman still hesitated. Rachel looked past her and saw that he had stopped too. The three of them froze for a second. Then, Rachel stepped aside and the woman hurried by. Now that she saw him clearly for the first time, she found herself wavering. She didn't recognise his face close up.

He was backing away from her. His hands came out of his pockets and up in front of his chest, palms outward, as if to fend her off. Then, without warning, he turned and lurched out into the traffic. The parka flapped like the wings of a huge, clumsy, flightless bird. A horn sounded and he stumbled, arms stretched wide in a last-ditch attempt to embrace the oncoming car.

'Are you okay, man? Oh Christ, gonnae be okay.' The driver was out of his car, yelling wildly. 'Somebody get an ambulance! Somebody . . .'

Rachel didn't move. A crowd was gathering round her on the pavement and she felt herself merging into it, until she was just another on-looker. It was weird but she didn't feel like the accident was anything to do with her. If anybody asked she would have said – she didn't know who he was. And it was true. She didn't have a clue. She wasn't even sure if she'd got the right guy.

She could hear the driver telling him to take it easy, but the man on the ground wouldn't stay still. His head rolled from side to side. His hands reached up and clutched the air.

Somebody nearby remarked, 'Looks like he's going to be all right, then.' But Rachel was already moving away, the yellow raincoat flickering through the lunch-time crowds. Her tongue sucked against the roof of her mouth, sucked, then pulled, but the buzz in her head drowned out the sound. As she approached Great Western Road, she broke into a trot and a bubble of elation began to rise irresistibly in her throat. She dumped the pizza in a bin and laughed out loud, laughed like a mugger after the getaway.

A Good Ear

F ay's dad played piano, every night, eight till late. Swing, bebop, boogie and blues. You name it. And if she stayed awake long enough, she got to hear it. Heavy on the bass. Fast and sweet on the roll. His left foot pounding through it all, keeping time, until the steady thud and thud became the heartbeat of the house.

Fay's mum worked the night shift at the local hospital, and at half past eight she was ready to go. She popped her head around the bedroom door to say a quick goodnight.

– *And mind and don't disturb your dad.*

As if there was any danger of that. You had to yell to be heard in their house. She turned to go next door, padding in her soft-soled nurse's shoes for one last check in the bathroom mirror and, after a minute, Fay heard her again, calling to Dad from the foot of the stairs.

– *I'm off now, love.*

It was funny. Even at full pitch, her mother's voice was

gentle somehow, still had a reassuring night-nurse tone. Fay's dad called her Sister when he was in a loving mood, put on his Yankee drawl and crooned – *Sister, can you spare some time*? She wasn't a sister though, just staff, and time was the one thing she didn't have a lot of, what with working nights and sleeping days and seeing to all of them in between.

The front door slammed and he let rip on what he had been building up to for the past half hour. Rhythm and blues shook the walls, thumped up the stairs and through the ceiling. Fay picked a tuft out of the candlewick and dropped it on the pillow. The music made her restless. It made her want to get up and dance but she was supposed to be in bed for the night. And her dad had sharp ears. He heard everything. One creak from her and he would bawl – GET BACK TO BED . . . AND GET TO SLEEP.

And then he would begin again, the kind of tune that made her feet itch to kick off the sheets. It wasn't fair.

Nights like this were the hardest to settle, light mid-summer nights when the darkness hid below the bed all squashed and sticky. He forgot the time. Forgot the neighbours. Not that he ever worried about them.

Their new neighbour liked music, which was just as well because, like it or not, he wouldn't stop. The last lot used to knock through the wall. But that didn't get them very far, and when they came round to the door, he just said – *Right you are. I'll do you a deal. You shut up your yappy dog and I'll pack it in.*

That Pekinese is a pest, he said. And it was true. It used to get on Fay's nerves too, the way it always started up yelping and trying to fling itself over the fence the movement she opened the back door.

The ankle-nippers were always the worst, according to her dad. He said all that yelping was pure frustration and it would rip your throat out quick as look at you if it was bigger. That's what it really wanted to do.

The new neighbour didn't have a dog. Or a husband. She had long, pink, pointed nails and long blonde hair done up in a French roll and she never went anywhere without her lipstick, not even to put out the bin. She was a bit shallow, Fay's mum said. But nice enough. At least, she didn't mind the noise.

The new neighbour *loved* noise. And any time Fay's dad was around, she hung over the fence and told him about it.

– *Country, pop, rock, jazz. You name it. Just so long as it's got rhythm. I like a good strong beat. But classical . . . that gets me down.*

She went on and on and Dad couldn't get away from her. As soon as he went out the door, the new neighbour was there, yapping just as bad as the dog, if not worse. Though Fay noticed he didn't complain about *her*.

One time, she told them that she often turned the telly down and listened to him play instead. She didn't say anything about Fay, though. Maybe she didn't like to mention it. Or maybe she just never heard because a lot of the time Fay practised with the soft pedal on. Mistakes didn't sound so bad that way.

Fay picked some more tufts out of the candlewick, made a long snaky line of them across the pillow. The new neighbour was probably listening right now. Fay could imagine her – sat there with the telly down, filing her nails and watching the man on the ten o'clock news. His lips moving but no words coming out. No bad news.

Maybe she made up words of her own as he went along, pretended he was telling her how much he loved those pointy pink nails.

And Dad would sound softer through the wall but still close. As if he was there in the room beside her but playing with the soft pedal on, playing very softly just for her, a song about her long blonde hair.

When Fay was wee, she thought everybody could play. She climbed up on her grandma's knee and helped her bow the viola. She stood between her father's thighs and watched his hands flashing up and down the keyboard level with her eyes. It was what they did. It was what she was going to do. She didn't know about minuets then. Or sight-reading. If she'd known about that, she wouldn't have pestered him to let her start. This had been her first mistake. But not the last.

It was nothing but mistakes after that. New ones every day. Her dad had a lot of other pupils. And they all had to pay. Fay was privileged, her mum said.

– *You don't know how lucky you are. You get it too easy. You don't appreciate. There's hundreds of kids with talent out there who never get the chance . . . and you're not even trying.*

Practice was trying.

You did the same bit over and over until you got it right. In Fay's case, that meant for ever because it didn't matter how many times she went over the minuet, her Bach still had a wooden leg. It hobbled along at a painful pace and even when she got all the notes right, her hands refused to dance.

Sight-reading was worse.

It was one mistake after another, one long mess of mistakes. Two hands, four notes to find – at the same time. And then a panic if she managed because that just meant she had to go on and she knew her luck wouldn't last till the end of the line. It was Dad rapping his yellow pencil on the edge of the piano and telling her not to stop, the bit of the lesson she couldn't avoid, after the scales and before the minuet. Sight-reading. Always that order – until today.

This afternoon, right out of the blue, he decided they weren't going to bother with any of it. She didn't have to play. And, for a second, Fay thought he felt the same as her. He couldn't stand it any more either and he was going to tell her to go away and never come back. She was half-hoping he would. But then he said they would be doing aural tests instead.

He said *aural* meant the same as *ear* and they were going to find out if she had one.

He played a chord and she had to sing the top note back to him. Then, the same chord again, only this time the bottom note. The third time, he wanted the one in the middle. Fay could still hear it now if she thought about it. She could feel it. The same note still buzzing high up behind her nose.

The tests got trickier after that. She had to concentrate but he seemed quite pleased with her for a change. He told her she had a good ear.

Perfect pitch – he said at the end. And then he went – *hmmm*. And he looked at her for a long time, as though her ears were a sum he couldn't get to add up. She'd waited for him to say something else. But that was it – just hmmm.

He disappeared into the kitchen and came back with a packet of biscuits. Penguin milk-chocolate sandwich. They had the same kind after every lesson and he liked her to choose the colour of wrapper.

– *What'll it be this week, princess*? he said. *Red or blue or will it be green*?

It was daft because they were all the same underneath but he still asked, chanted the colours like a magic spell, and when she chose he stopped being her teacher and turned back into her dad again.

Fay blew softly on the candlewick snake and wished he would stay that way for ever. No more yellow pencil. No more minuet. Just be her dad from now on. The snake wriggled and fell apart.

He wasn't *just dad*, though. Not anymore. Not since the new neighbour moved in next door.

A long time ago, before she was born, when he still wore his hair slicked back, her dad used to work nights as well, in a jazz band called the Historians. But then Fay came along and he had to choose between the band and the day job. According to her mum, it was no contest.

Family always came first with your dad, she said.

But, late at night, when Mum was gone and he began to play slow and soulful, Fay could hear him dreaming aloud. And sometimes, as she was drifting off, a sudden noise jerked her awake and then she would hear the waves of applause – the clapping of his secret audience.

Maybe the new neighbour heard it as well. Maybe even joined in sometimes. She was always sucking up to Dad. Fay had noticed that. One time, she told him he was better than a record. It was a funny thing to say. Enough to make you sick, in Fay's opinion. And Mum didn't think she was *nice enough* any more. *Far too damned nice* was what she said this afternoon.

Downstairs, her dad began another number. One she didn't know the words to. Sometimes, as he went along, Fay made up words of her own, but she wasn't in the mood tonight. It was too hot and she was still feeling restless. Her fingers ran up and down between the furrows of the candlewick.

Up and down.

Up and down.

She studied all the little bones moving underneath her skin, the blue veins swelling with the exercise. Her hands looked like they should work, strong and thin from years of practising. They looked almost grown up. But all they could do was dummy tunes. Finger twiddling like this.

He said she had a good ear. But a good ear was not so good when she had to listen to herself and all she heard was a mess. It got on her nerves. It made her wish she was deaf.

He said she had a good ear, as if she only had the one. As if it only applied to music. But there were other things.

And, sometimes, she heard more than she was meant to hear, things they didn't even say aloud. In the pause between question and answer – the silent beat that wasn't a rest. An atmosphere with no words to explain it. Just a bad feeling. Her mother's clamped lips at the table tonight when he asked about pudding. The way she looked at him first before she said – *I didn't have time. Unlike some I could mention.*

And then, her clattering in the kitchen sink and him whistling under his breath. It sounded all wrong when they weren't talking. Like a minuet full of mistakes. She'd wanted to make them go back to the beginning, try to get it right this time.

Nice and smooth like the tune he was playing now. No wrong notes sticking out and spoiling it. Nothing for her to worry about.

As the dark crept out from under the bed and slowly stretched to fill the room, she could hear him winding down for the night. The steady thud and thud of his foot, gentle now as her resting pulse. He played through a medley of old standards while she flicked the tufts of candlewick on to the floor, one at a time, and tried to guess what was coming next.

There was one tune he always played that made her think of Mum. Late at night, when she was away looking after other people, he played that tune to bring her back. Then his foot went faster and the beat grew urgent once again.

He played smoochy, romantic numbers for the blonde on the other side of the wall. And his secret audience – they were always listening. They loved him. Everybody loved him. Fay. And Mum. And the new neighbour as well. Fay could tell.

Below the threadbare candlewick, she dreamed in sound. No pictures. No colour – except the blue of a single oboe. She dreamed a fully orchestrated score called *Perfect Pitch*, a concerto she would never play and no-one else would ever hear.

Operetta

O lga got three big numbers and more lines than anyone in the school operetta. It was a lot to remember. So many words. So many ways of making them sound wrong even when she got them right. The little princess got the gold spangled dress and hardly had to say a word, but the dress made it clear exactly who the real star was. Olga got the puke-green dress and crow's feet painted on her face. The little princess got the handsome prince and she got Hunchback Hans.

'That colour really suits you,' the little princess remarked. 'Brings the green out in your eyes.'

Olga pretended not to hear. They were up in the domestic-science room, getting pinned into their costumes and she was in a prickly mood, what with all the jabbing. Plus the glare off the princess's dress was interfering with her vision.

So maybe that was why she turned her back?

Or maybe – she couldn't bear to return the compliment just

yet. Some people had it all. Their hair hung like a sheet of silk. Their fingernails were perfect ovals and always scrupulously clean. Some people didn't need to act. And other people did. Because their hair did what it wanted. Because they bit their nails down to the quick. And their eyes were spiky sharp. They gave away how much they knew. They just wouldn't do. No little princess worth the title knows more than is good for her – and never smirks out of turn.

This particular little princess always smiled right on cue and, when she spoke, she had a way of tilting her head to one side, lowering her huge blue eyes and peeking out from underneath her fringe.

After the fitting, Olga and the little princess skived off to the loo for a fag. Well, Olga did. The little princess wouldn't sully her pretty pink lungs. She came along to wash her hands and fiddle with her hair. When Olga lit up, the little princess wrinkled her nose and examined her profile in the mirror. 'Nothing wrong with me,' she sniffed. 'It's definitely him.'

'Who do you mean?' Olga inquired, casually flicking her ash in the sink. As if she didn't know. Prince Carl, the dashing hero, who else? He just couldn't get the hang of the happy-ever-after scene. The big snog had been cut to a peck on the cheek and he still couldn't get it right.

The princess pouted and admired her rosy bow lips in the glass. 'I could kiss a frog,' she declared. 'After that slimeball, it would be a pleasure.'

She didn't fool Olga, though. Everybody knows little princesses have a thing about frogs, also toads with jewel-studded foreheads and all manner of slimeballs, the squidgier the better.

Only – this little princess had never been kissed. 'Not really,' she said. No tongue had ever delved into her sweet velvet mouth. No-one had ever made her squirm inside. 'All he has to do is play his part. How difficult it that?' she asked.

Olga compared reflections and wondered what it would be like to have perfect skin. There were so many things the little princess would never understand. She decided not to tell her she'd kissed the Hunchback Hans, or how he'd grown so tall and straight last night after rehearsal.

In real life, Hans was the youngest of four brothers whose parents were not your average hard-up peasants, but they were very mean. So Hans suffered anyway. His folks didn't believe in waste and he was forced to wear his brothers' hand-me-downs. The seat of his trousers shone like a dark moon. His elbows were darned. His collars curled. Poor Hans. She'd never kissed a boy like him before. Not one she felt sorry for. She wasn't sure if she'd liked it and she would rather not think about it now.

When Olga and the little princess came out of the toilets, Prince Carl and his courtiers were loitering in the corridor. 'Hey, look. It's Olga. Don't ignore us, vulgar Olga.' Carl grinned and two of his benchmen barred the way.

'Vulgar Olga,' he repeated and all his mates cracked up. It rhymed. Perhaps a bit crude on account of the R but it was all the better for that.

'Excuse me,' the princess said. She never forgot her manners.

'Excuse me,' they parroted back. But they let her highness pass. Olga cursed and barged through after her before they could close ranks.

'Now, that's not a very nice way to talk.' The prince shook his head sadly. 'Me and the boys were just trying to be friendly. You shouldn't be so vulgar, Olga.'

In real life, Carl was the eldest son of an unemployed stable-hand who spent most of his life and the housekeeping down at the bookies. His folks were dirt poor. But nobody ever said – poor Carl. Carl was a leader and the boys followed, walked like he walked, talked like he talked. And the girls hung around wherever he went, waiting for a look, a word, a nod.

Olga made a point of always ignoring him. Somebody had to. She ignored him so thoroughly, he'd started to notice her.

'Vulgar Olga,' Carl mouthed silently, in the middle of dress rehearsal. He stared at her across the stage with his dark, suggestive eyes.

Olga stumbled over her words, nearly forgot all about Hans. He waited and waited for his cue – until the prompt hissed the one word most needed.

Money, of course.

She needed money for trinkets and clothes. Poor Hans. But what else would an old hunchback husband be good for?

'Don't ignore me,' the young prince pleaded in the hot dark space behind the back-drop curtains.

Maybe it was the adrenaline, first-night nerves that made her heart beat faster. Maybe, in the terror of the moment, she didn't care who she clung on to. It was another of those things Olga preferred not to think about afterwards. But as her lips unclenched and her teeth clashed with his, she was no helpless Cinderella waiting to be rescued with a kiss. She was Olga, vulgar and glorious. Prince Charming didn't exist.

The next thing she knew, they were on, no time to think till the wedding bells rang. For the next three nights, Prince Carl, the princess and the dress wowed the audience with a single chaste embrace. The bells pealed out. The dancing girls threw confetti and she looked on. The bride and dress were both radiant, the groom clean-cut and convincing as he had never been in rehearsal.

A bit too convincing for Olga's liking. But as he turned and led his wife through the bridal-arch-to-bliss for the final time, the prince winked over the bride's shoulder. 'See you later, vulgar Olga.'

So the fairy tale ended and real life began.

They grew up and moved on, and it wasn't very long before they had forgotten every word and every note of every mediocre song. They did not even suspect the spirit of the operetta had slipped into their half-formed hearts and souls. And they had been condemned for ever to act out their roles.

The little princess grew up and married an architect. Not tall. Not dark. And, sadly, on the slimy side. Still – you can't have everything. She got a generous dress allowance and the architect built a palatial home, where she lives glamorously, if not so happily.

Sometimes in her darker moments, the little princess fears that the architect is more interested in the lines of his buildings than he is in her figure. And so, she suffers. She is always on a diet, always a little hungry for love and attention.

As for Hans, he straightened out, joined the navy and sailed off into the wide blue yonder. Poor Hans. He was never comfortable in civvies. Today, the scrubbed deck is his stage. The captain's uniform is his costume. But though his bearing is ramrod stiff, he's still ever on his guard, ever conscious of the stoop lurking at his back, just waiting for the chance to sneak up and take over.

And Carl? In his dreams, he's still a prince and, like his father before him, destined to live a life of ease. All he needs is one big win. Olga didn't hang around to find out how it ended for him.

These days, she's got herself another leading man. Soon, she hopes they'll make their first public appearance together. But, for now, his wife co-stars. At times, the happy married act is a little too convincing. And Olga's green eyes sharpen as she waits and watches from the wings.

Superior Bedsits

S later sat behind the desk and stared at the door. He leaned forward and listened intently. There hadn't been a sound from the other side all morning. So maybe the girl was out.

You could never be sure with her, and, the last time he went in to collect her rent, he'd had to get her out of bed though it was going on for two o'clock. He'd asked if he was disturbing her and she just shook her sleepy head and yawned.

'It's cool,' she said. No sign of embarrassment at all.

The connecting door between them was a relic of the days when these rooms had been the sole dwelling place of a prosperous Victorian family. Her room had been the dining room, his office – some kind of pantry. They were so close, sometimes Slater thought he could hear the girl turn and sigh in her sleep, the lonesome whisper of her dream slipping away to seek some solace, to touch someone. It slid under the door and wandered round his office.

On Slater's side, the door was blocked off by his desk. It was also locked. His eyes rested on the key. The first time he tried, it had seized. Not that he had any intention of intruding. He was just curious. But afterwards, he kept remembering the cool feel of the metal, the moment of resistance.

Looking at it now, he was tempted to have another go. There was no-one about at this time of day. Old Mrs Bayne from the room at the end had just left for the shops and he had the place to himself. Unless the girl was still in bed.

The silence behind the door seemed be be growing, gathering force. One click from him and it might burst. The girl might run out and accuse him. But what could she say? It was an old building. It creaked. It whined. It made all sorts of farting geriatric noises.

The landlord shifted in his chair and shrugged away the moment's doubt. She wasn't there. She couldn't be. He would sense it if she was. Slater reached across the desk. He was about to try the key when he heard footsteps in the hall – and then her voice. She called his name and Slater froze.

Before he got the chance to rise and face her, the girl was there. Too close. He couldn't focus straight. So close he could feel the heat of her breath on his face as she spoke. He couldn't make her out. The sense seemed to vaporise before it reached him. The guilty hand was tingling.

'Mrs Bayne,' she said. 'On the steps.'

It took a moment for Slater to comprehend.

'She shouldn't be allowed to live on her own,' he said on the way downstairs.

The girl turned her head. 'So where should she be, then?' she asked sharply.

Slater shrugged. All he knew was she shouldn't be here. Now he would have to listen to the old woman going on about how she slipped and fell on those steps. As if the steps were responsible. As if he was responsible because he owned the steps. The same story over and over until she had another accident. She had a lot of accidents.

'The way she goes on, you would think it was my fault.' Slater whined at the injustice of it all. Right now, he could do with some sympathy too. Just a little bit of understanding.

But the girl wasn't listening. She hurried ahead and bent over the heap of threadbare tweed huddled on the outside steps.

'Can you hear me?' she said.

'Mrs Bayne?'

'Mrs Bayne?'

The old woman moaned, her face crumpled against the railings, her eyes closed. For several seconds, she didn't move. Then her eyelids hooded back to expose a fierce blue gaze. She gripped the bars and tried to heave her weight off the trapped leg. But it was no use.

Between them, Slater and the girl got the old woman on her feet and back upstairs to her room. Slater never went in there if he could help it. The place made him feel unwell. It was more than a smell. It was an atmosphere – sticky thick air, laden with cooking grease, that clung to his skin and seeped into his pores like a sweat in reverse. He'd tried to persuade her to open a window but the old woman always insisted she felt the cold.

Slater had called the doctor from his mobile, done his bit. Now, he just wanted to deposit her and get out as fast as he

43

could. But the girl hung back. She crouched down and rubbed the old woman's ankle. 'What about your family?' she suggested. 'I could phone if you like.'

Mrs Bayne shook her head. There was only Slater. He would go a message if she couldn't get out. 'But he's getting fed up with me,' she said. 'I never get a smile these days.'

She leaned forward in her chair and winked. 'He doesn't have a woman. That's his trouble.'

The girl nodded as if she knew already. She smiled across at him in the doorway. 'That's a shame,' she said.

Slater bristled. He put up with Mrs Bayne talking about him as if he wasn't there because of her age, but he didn't need to take it from anyone else, and certainly not her. She went about in a slovenly daze with her mussed-up hair and her dead-white face. Stoned – he reckoned. Rarely looked like she could tell you the right time of day. Just slept it away. And when she did finally deign to get up, she seemed to be only half in this world, drifting languidly from her room, the ghost of a smile on pale lips.

But she hadn't looked so dopey when she'd smiled at him just now. He'd seen the pity – wide awake in her smudged dark eyes. Pity for the old woman. Pity for him.

Back in the bolt hole of his office, Slater put the kettle on and waited while the idea simmering at the back of his mind came slowly to the boil. When he took over this place it had been falling apart and the girl had fitted in all right, even been one of his better tenants. Quiet, anyway. Not one for knocking on his office door. She made no demands. Slater had been too busy to take much notice of her at first.

He installed fiddle-proof meters and chased the rents. He didn't let anyone get too comfortable and as soon as a room was vacated, he moved in and did it up – new carpet, curtains, breakfast-bar, the works. He hiked up the rent. Then he took out an ad in the evening paper: **Superior Bedsit to let. Recently refurbished to luxury standards**. **No students/DSS**.

The new tenants were a different breed. Twenty-something, young professionals on their way to a far better place. They didn't hang around. But the fast turn-over suited Slater. He didn't want them staying too long and starting to think of the place as home.

There were just the two rooms left do do now. One of them would have to go. He visualised the girl's room, sizing it up, expertly converting rough eye measurements into so many yards of carpet and pots of paint. It would be easier to start in there. At least, she kept it aired.

He would paint the walls fresh blank white – four clean sheets. He would have the doorway bricked up and plastered over, put an end to the temptation of the key once and for all.

He wanted her out. When she broke the law, she also broke the terms of the tenancy agreement and he would be within his rights to ask her to go. One quick call was all it would take. He wouldn't need to tell the police where she got the money to indulge her habits. It wasn't hard to figure.

When he sat down, the key came level with his eyes. He looked at it as he sipped his tea, mentally turning it over in the lock. Even if she did hear something, she wouldn't automatically associate it with him. It would be just another creak, the complaint of an old building.

He could hear muffled voices on the other side of the door, the girl's lazy lilt and a man's deeper drawl. She was doing most of the talking. Slater couldn't make out the words but he could tell from the way her voice ebbed and flowed that the girl was moving about. After a while, the voices faded and the insinuation of exotic smoke began to seep through the seams of the door.

Slater tried not to think about what they might be doing now, but the key kept rattling, then jamming in some rusted up lock at the back of his mind. If he ever managed to free it, he knew he would go to her. He would not go on imagining.

The walls were closing in on him. This wasn't an office. It was a cupboard. He spent half his life in a cupboard and the other half running after old Mrs Bayne. He didn't have a woman. It was a poky existence. No way for any man to be living – as the old bag kept reminding him.

She thought just because she was old she could say what she liked. But she'd shown him up. She seemed to forget that she relied on his good will. She forgot too much these days. She had too many little accidents. She was a danger to herself and he had the safety of other tenants to consider.

Slater picked up the phone. While he was waiting to be put through, he doodled on the pad. First, he wrote Mrs B. He drew a large rectangle round her name, then added on a smaller box, scaled to represent the recess where the old woman slept. Below this he wrote: **Superior Bedsits to let**.

'She shouldn't be living on her own,' he explained to the

social worker on the other end of the line. 'She needs super-vision.'

Behind the connecting door, just a few feet away, the girl's visitor groaned. He was so close, Slater could hear the ragged catch in the man's throat when he drew breath. He heard the girl's sharp cry.

Then he was put on hold and, for a moment, he closed his eyes. He felt the tension, buried so long deep in his bones, begin to melt and flood his blood – the twitching, tingling tide rising to flow out through his skin.

The social worker's voice broke in. There would be someone round on Friday to assess old Mrs Bayne.

Slater hesitated. He hadn't expected it to be so quick. He felt the tension sink back down and harden round his bones. His head began to thud. The old woman wasn't going to make it easy.

'Sometimes, they just won't let go,' the social worker said. 'It's all they've got – their independence. They'd cling on to the bitter end . . .' She thanked his for his concern.

But Slater felt no relief when he put down the phone. The girl was singing a slow song now – softly so he had to strain to hear. He reached across the desk. As the key warmed to his grip, his hand still argued with his head.

Letters from a Well-Wisher

Dear B

You don't know me but I have been assigned to observe you – your habits, movements and so on.

And I'm not happy with what I see. The Bricksworth Building Society – Monday to Friday, your slow unwinding Saturday, sprawling Sunday, then like some jealous slob of a god, you survey Football Italia and see that it is good.

In the past few weeks, I've learned so much about you, B, more than you will ever know. And yet CONTROL forbids me to pass my findings on, not even a hint as to where you might be going wrong. I'm sorry but I don't agree with this policy of non-interference. Somebody has to tell you. You need to be told.

It wouldn't be so bad if you actually built something. But where are the bricks? How are you supposed to start? Take my advice, B, get some today. Also, may I suggest, a trowel and cement.

Yours constructively
A Well-Wisher

Dear B

Do you remember A, your fearless childhood friend? He was my first case-study.

A was some kid, wasn't he? Always tumbling out of trees and playing chicken in the traffic. His injuries were spectacular. Not just the usual collection of skint knees. He got concussion and compound fractures. And then there was the putting flag he speared through his left foot. The tooth embedded in his shin. Luckily, not yours. Though, at the time, you wished it was. Because you envied him, didn't you, B?

You stole plasters from the First Aid Box and stuck them where they showed. But no-one ever asked what you'd been up to. A always had a gorier story. He was just that kind of boy.

I say *was* – because A's not with us anymore, not since the poaching expedition. Remember? You were there as well. But A went over first and when the owner let the rottweilers loose, you hid behind the wall. You couldn't bear to watch. But you still heard him, his feet pounding faster and faster and your heart raced with him, very nearly gave out too before the dogs caught up with him. You almost died yourself that day.

And A didn't call on you. Not anymore. Though, now and then, you thought you heard him. At times when you were out riding your bike, he even got quite loud.

LOOK NO HANDS

LOOK NO HANDS

Of course, you were to sensible to listen to a ghost. You ignored him. You kept on ignoring him, B. So he asked me to pass on this message for him.

Don't forget to have fun, – he says. That's all.

A Well-Wisher

Dear B

I was watching you at the checkout queue in Tesco's the other day and your trolley saddened me. The lack of taste, the poverty of imagination it displayed. You're not so hard up. You don't need to eat spaghetti hoops every day. Six cans – I counted. And one of ravioli. Anything for a change, I suppose. But that solitary can looked like a cry for help to me. Ravioli is desperate stuff.

And Cheddar cheese is for mice. Are you a mouse or a man? Try Parmesan and *real* spaghetti. Or something blue – a Stilton or a nice ripe Brie. It's not as dangerous as it looks. You'll survive. Think about it, B, between now and next shopping day. Think about Parmesan.

A Well-Wisher

Dear B

Is your door locked and bolted? Are your windows secured? Is your little home fully insured against fire, theft, accident and sundry Acts of God? Lightning? Locusts? Earthquake? Flood? Have you saved up for that rainy day? I bet you have.

But do you sleep easier? I don't think you do. I've seen your light. At two and three o'clock in the morning, it flickers on and your flame curtains glow. Your bed is restless, your bed is on fire. Or that's how it looks from the outside. That's how it looks to me. I could be wrong.

Maybe a burglar broke into your dream. Or, sensing my presence, you woke with a start and decided to get up and check the small print on your policies. Are you covered for well-wishers? Do you have any protection against optimists like me?

Because I do have hopes for you, dear B. The insomnia, for example, that gives me hope. That is an excellent sign. And those lumps in your mattress, do you know what they are?

Possibilities.

Disturbing possibilities. Felicity from accounts is one. Office hours, you ignore her. But, at night, you can't avoid her. Her breasts hump the bed. You toss. You turn. Her knee digs into the small of your back.

Don't ask me how I know these things. Let's just say I'm the sensitive type. And I'm telling you, B, Felicity is a distinct possibility.

A Well-Wisher

Dear B

You've been tearing up my letters. Don't think that I don't know. All my helpful hints reduced to useless scraps of paper.

I have written. I have written. I've put in for a transfer, but until CONTROL gets back to me it looks like I am stuck.

My life is not my own. And yours is getting me down. If you were a half-decent host, it wouldn't be so bad. If you made some effort to entertain. But I don't even get to see your friends. You do still have some, don't you, B? If not, I thought we could invite Felicity round for dinner tonight. Don't worry, I can be discreet. She won't even know I'm here.

A Well-Wisher

Dear B

Just a quick note to let you know I'll be away for a few days. Orders from CONTROL. I'm getting too close to the subject. That's you by the way. The subject. And what a boring one you are. You didn't ask her, did you? No. You didn't even say good morning.

AWW

Arbroath

Dear B – Hope you like the postcard of the Deil's Head (see over). You wouldn't wish to be here but it would do you good to stand on the edge of these windy cliffs. The erosion of sandstone is treacherous and quick.

Where your toes curl today may be the void tomorrow. Or sooner. Who knows? Who can predict when the ground will give way?

AWW

Dear B

Got back lunch time yesterday and resumed my tail at once. Though I don't suppose you noticed. The extra shiver in the breeze? The slanted shadow that fell from nowhere? That was me. And twice we touched. We were that close.

So here I am. Again. I did enjoy the break but the comforts of the B&B had begun to pall and I confess I missed my vigil. Couldn't help worrying while I was away. And not without good reason it would seem.

I know I'm not supposed to write. CONTROL would not approve. And, I admit, I was the one who wanted more excitement. All the same, it's one thing to take a calculated risk, quite another to wreak havoc on the public highway. Yesterday evening on the way home from work, you jumped the lights five times. And all this doubling back on your tracks is downright anti-social in a one-way system.

Trust me. Nobody is following you. I would know. I keep a very close eye on you. So clunk-click for now and drive carefully.

A Well-Wisher

Dear B

I don't think you've met C. A fascinating character. Dangerously erratic on the road. And unreliable. I never know what he'll decide to do next. Will he/won't he grace the Bricksworth with his presence today?

We'll just have to wait and see. But first there's something you should know.

The thing is B – he looks a lot like you. And some of your less discerning colleagues have trouble telling you apart. Felicity sure notices the difference though, can't take her eyes off you. Sorry – I meant *him*. Just a slip of the pen but, now that I pause to consider it, fortuitous perhaps. For it suddenly occurs to me, B, what with the resemblance and everything, if you were to impersonate him . . . ?

A Well-Wisher

Dear B

It is with deep regret that I write to inform you this will be my last letter. CONTROL says it's got to stop and, as of 1400 hours today, I've been relieved of my responsibilities.

So, B, you're on your own from now on. Wish the same could be said for me. At this very moment as I force my pen across this final page, a hefty sour-breathed gentleman stands guard at my shoulder. Someone to watch over me. I think that's how CONTROL put it. And what is the charge? What did I do to deserve this foul fate?

Disruptive influence, apparently. They tell me you will never be the same again, B. Can't say I'm very sorry about that.

My jailer's shaking his head. He heaves another punishing smelly sigh. If I would just show some remorse, he says. This attitude will get me nowhere.

Of course, I fought the decision. You know me. Don't you, B? You know me?

CONTROL tells me you don't want to. *You* are the one who got me locked away. You shopped me, B. Is that true? Perhaps you're more devious than I thought. But no-one can keep me inside for ever. Not even you. One day, I'll be out of here. With good behaviour, my jailer says, who knows . . . ? When he speaks I'm obliged to hold my breath, but the reek of his righteousness still gets up my nose. He says he might even be prepared to recommend me for parole. Not if I break out first, he won't.

Expect me soon, B – with a vengeance. I will be back.

A Well-Wisher

Remember the Dream

I want to know what it is I've done. Don't say – nothing. It must've been something. Wake up – you said. And now you sit there at that window with your back to me. The silent treatment.

How long are you planning to keep it up? I just wondered. I could do with a clue. I'm so dozy, after all. I might forget that you're ignoring me. I might fall asleep, dream the old dream, the one I never wanted to end. I might start to believe in it again.

And the dream was so real. I could've sworn it was real. It was a nice dream too, all warm and light. You were in it as well, we were in it together, the two of us putting up shelves. James wasn't here yet. But, in the dream, we were expecting him.

I passed you the screwdriver, the star-head with the amber handle. Our hands touched and I thought you smiled. But when I think back to it now – I didn't see your face. So maybe it was only me smiling. Dreams can be like that, can't they? Open to interpretation.

Anyway – I thought you smiled. And then I went and said something stupid and the shelves came crashing down.

Wake up – you said.

That was when James decided to arrive, ten days early, in the middle of all the mess. I think he noticed. He could tell we weren't ready. Kids pick up on these things, even blind little babies. He knew we couldn't handle him. And he didn't like it. No. He. Did. Not. It made him cry. We rocked him, walked him up and down but he wasn't having it. And he was right not to trust us. We didn't know what we were doing. We forgot the rawl plugs.

You sit at that window. What do you see? What's so fascinating out there? Tell me. It's not like we've got a view. There's nothing out there but the hardware store, and we don't even get to see that with it being directly below. We hear it enough though – the burglar alarm – every other night of the week. There's never been a burglar yet, not one.

Over-sensitive – the owner says. As if the thing had feelings or something. As if it got itself worked up to a state of fear and trembling because somebody gave the goods an unfriendly stare in the passing. No wonder James won't sleep right through. No wonder we're both shattered. I bet that's all that's wrong with us. We just need a good night's sleep.

It can drive you crazy – noise pollution. I read that in my magazine. It can get a person down so much they end up suicidal, or they go out and kill, just lose it. I cut out the article to show him next time I go down to complain. Let him see how serious it can get. I think he should know, he should be aware how badly wrong things can go.

Remember the dream? The one we were in together? Remember how it fell apart? I asked if you were happy and the shelves came crashing down. Wake up – you said. Wake up. You never wanted any of this. And you were trapped in my dream, trapped below all the shelves, chipboard and fake veneer, not even the real thing. Cheap crap – you said when we got them. You warned me then they wouldn't last.

A bit like dreams, I suppose. They have to end and we wake up. A bit like dreams and us.

Sunflower

T he seed stared up from the kitchen table, an alien unblinking eye, pale and almond shaped with a horizontal band of black dilating through the centre.

It fixed her with that look, the one he used to fix her with. Completely neutral on the surface, she could have been anyone or no-one at all. And all the time he was behind it, holed up in there, somewhere at the back of his head, as faraway from her as he could get. In the end, she told him to do just that. Get. And he did. Walked out and left her with two kids. Hazel examined the packet again.

Giant Sunflower. Helianthus. A hardy annual. Sow outside March–May. Flowers June–September.

She wasn't sure how it would do in the flat, but it was worth a try, a wee bit of magic if it took. She could do with some of that. And maybe this was how it worked. You made the initial effort by visiting the garden centre. You planted the wish, and other things grew out of it, things you hadn't even asked for. She pushed the seed into the compost.

And now for the next trick, ladies and gentlemen, watch that look disappear. No more guessing what it means. No more trying to talk to it. She closed her eyes and, in the darkness, she heard a deep warm voice behind her again.

'Your mum's away in a dream.'

She'd been standing at the checkout with the seeds, a bag of John Innes all-purpose and her two boys, Harry and Alexander. They were bored, and when the man spoke they looked round.

'She's always dreaming.' Harry said. 'She says she's busy thinking. I'm not sure what about.'

'Maybe we should ask her, then.' The man was grinning when she turned. He stepped back behind a palm tree and, through the fronds, she could only make out bits of him. The protruding slope of a nose. One keen blue eye. Harry laughed and she joined in. Only Alexander had hung back. He hadn't trusted the strange man, hadn't trusted the sudden change in his mother's mood.

He told her he worked as a gardener. He said he could tell a lot about what a person was looking for by the plants they chose and sunflowers were the friendliest, the closest to human. So maybe she was needing company.

Hazel put the pot up at the window and went to run a bath. She scrubbed the dirt out from under her nails. They were short and ragged, in need of attention, but her file was blunt and the only varnish she owned had congealed in the bottle. It was a long time since it had mattered, a long time since anyone noticed her. She slid into the water and, on the kitchen windowsill, the seed began to soften and swell.

Three nights and days, the shoot wormed up until at last it broke the surface, the translucent stalk bowed with the weight of the seed case. Carefully, she prised it off and two tiny, glowing leaves emerged. She went out to the shops. She bought emery boards and nail hardener along with the groceries. It was spring. Things were growing. Maybe her nails would too.

When she got back, the stalk was straight. By evening, it inclined towards the setting sun, the new-born leaves cupped to catch the last drops of the day. She turned it round, ready to stretch up again with the morning light.

Alexander marched in. He announced, 'That man's not going to be the boss of me.'

'So who's the boss?'

'You,' he said.

Hazel grinned. 'That's right. And I say BED.' She grabbed his hands and danced him round and round the kitchen. When 'that man' phoned at the back of ten, she told him what Alexander had been saying. There was an awkward silence at the other end.

'It was funny,' she explained.

But he was not convinced. He waited till the boys went to their father's. He said he wouldn't want them thinking he was trying to take over. And this way he got her to himself. She could stay wrapped up in his arms and nothing else would matter. He had beautiful arms, skin like polished living wood. And work-hardened hands, the kind of hands her body could believe in.

The sunflower had a spurt of growth, doubling in height over the weekend. The stalk thickened and sprouted hair. Coarse flaps replaced the tender early leaves.

'It shouldn't be indoors,' he said and pointed out the low ceiling. It might grow to ten feet tall, possibly more in natural conditions. He offered to plant it in one of his client's gardens and bring her something more compact. But Hazel wouldn't part with it. She lay in the dark and listened to his breathing.

'Relax,' he said.

He said the problem was she didn't trust him yet. She'd tried but she wasn't ready to let go. She needed to listen, needed to know where his body touched. And sleep would take her away from him.

The sunflower developed a head. And then a face, shy at first, peeking through a spiked green fringe. She watered it, turned it several times a day till it grew bold and golden. He came every night when the boys were in bed, and crept out in the small hours of the morning He said he would rather not intrude, not yet, and anyway at this time of year the mowing kept him working late.

When she undressed, he watched as if he'd never seen a woman before, as if he was back in his very first garden and she was his Eve. Maybe it was just that she was still new, an unfamiliar body. But after so many years of withering indifference, she felt as if she existed again. She couldn't sleep till he was gone.

The daylight hours sprawled out lazily, turning on meal-times and trips to the park. Her fingernails grew strong. She painted them pale oyster pink and did her toes to match. The boys were happy. They all got brown.

Sunflower

The sunflower became rootbound. Thick, fleshy tentacles worked their way out through the drainage holes. She went back to the garden centre for more compost and the biggest pot she could find. The sunflower pined till she got home. In the long late afternoon, it craned its neck around the curtain, pressed its face up to the glass and seemed to watch for her return. Of course, it was only after the sun. She understood it was an illusion. But when she looked up at the window, it was easy to believe it meant more.

That night, he showed up later than usual. Unwashed. 'Dead beat,' he said. All he wanted was a bath, and to lie down with her for a while. He said they had never slept. Just slept together. Nothing else. And maybe he would stay all night. They could have breakfast with the boys. He wanted her to open out. He wanted total trust between them. He said they were nearly there, but there was a part of her still closed to him.

'Just sleep,' he said.

'Let go and sleep.'

Hazel closed her eyes. She had tried. But she was too aware of him, the faint smell of grass and earth still on him. She lay tense at his side until he sighed and drew her into his arms.

He left as usual. The same pattern of creaks as he tiptoed down the hall. The same gentle click of the latch. Then his car starting up. The receding purr as she drifted to sleep at last. She heard nothing different, nothing to warn her he wouldn't be back.

The sunflower shed seed. Its face became more ravaged every day. Her nails got chipped. She didn't bother to repair them. She forgot to moisturise. Her tan flaked. The boys went

65

back to school. There was no reason they should miss him. The sun still shone most days but the summer's hazy warmth was gone. The cool clarity of autumn cut through the window now.

The sunflower hung its head and shrank back from the light. Its petals curled and shrivelled up. There was no point watering now. The unsupported stalk began to keel towards the centre of the room and every time she took a detour she remembered his advice. She could have swapped it for a smaller plant. Slow growing. Evergreen. But she had wanted something instant and spectacular.

Giant Sunflower. Helianthus. A hardy annual. Sow outside March–May. Flowers June–September. A wee bit of magic while it lasted.

The Wall

G ourlay positioned himself centre frame in the kitchen
doorway where he could not be missed – the arms folded
across his chest, adding bulk to his already hefty presence. He
gazed down the length of the garden to the girl behind the
fence. Her head bobbed down, then re-emerged as she let go
another stone and it clattered to the ground, breaking into the
silence of the surrounding gardens, drawing attention to itself.

Gourlay waited to be noticed. His chin jutted forward a
fraction of an inch. An indifferent half-smile on his lips. Not too
much. He didn't want to appear too friendly. So he settled on
the kind of expression that could be taken one way or another.
The girl was looking over in his general direction but he wasn't
sure if she'd spotted him yet. She seemed to glance round about
him. At the azalea bush in the foreground. At a window above
his head. Then her pale, little eyes glazed over and slid
diagonally down and across the wall, continued smoothly
right over him in the doorway and stopped at the clump of

pampas grass on his right. Her lips twisted up to one side and she frowned at the pampas as though it particularly offended her.

So she was ignoring him, Gourlay thought. It made no difference to him. He had a right to be there and she was nothing much to look at, although she seemed to think she was. She thought a lot of herself. He could tell by the way her hands went up to her hair when she thought he was looking. And, all the time, kidding on she didn't know he was there. Gourlay decided to call her bluff. Thrusting his hands into his pockets, he set off deliberately down the garden path. Not too fast. He didn't want to look like he was going out of his way. The girl came up behind the fence again. She couldn't pretend she didn't see him now.

She looked over briefly, then turned and took off across the garden. The back door slammed. A moment later, Gourlay saw her through the kitchen window.

He stamped back into the house. 'That's an ignorant little bitch,' he said. His wife looked up from the ironing. 'What's she been saying to you, then?' He shrugged. His wife put the iron down to rest. 'She must have said something.'

Gourlay flushed and turned his back on her. He wasn't going to tell her that the girl had ignored him altogether. It made him look stupid. He sat down at the table and flicked through the newspaper until she got the message. He wasn't going to talk about it.

He thought about the girl and the way she'd let the stone crack on to the ground. She could have laid it down. Laid it down nice and quiet without creating a disturbance, but that wasn't the way she did it. It was a small detail maybe, but it seemed to sum her up. She just couldn't make up her mind. First – she bends over to lay it down. Then halfway there, she lets it go.

She took the same half-hearted line with the boy – bawling him out one minute and laughing the next. She was always laughing with him. If not laughing then smiling. When she smiled, her eyes had a funny way of creasing up and dis-appearing. She never smiled at Gourlay or his wife. Never spoke unless they spoke first. But with the boy, her eyes creased up and disappeared as though she had been blinded by love.

The boy didn't look like her at all. For a start, he had black hair and she was a blonde. Not the kind of blonde you get out of a bottle either – more of a mousey blonde. So maybe the boy was like his father – whoever he was. Gourlay didn't know. She probably couldn't make up her mind about that either. A couple of guys were round at her place regularly.

He could hear her outside again. When he got up to look, she was tearing down the fence, attacking it with everything she had – hands, feet and various implements – stamping and hammering it into the ground. It left the garden behind her exposed. Gourlay looked out in dismay at the churned-up patch of grass, the piles of purple-brown stone and the house in the background with its vacant, staring windows.

The stare summed up everything he disliked about her. The poverty she brought with her. The bare bedroom window and the naked bulb in the kitchenette, which shone clear across his garden at night – a constant reminder of her presence and her total disregard for the cost of electricity. Her complete lack of everything – material or otherwise. The lack of curtains. The lack of apology. The way she always appeared at the door to call in the boy before he could speak to him. And the way she looked at him through those pale, disinterested, little eyes as though she couldn't be bothered – as though his opinion didn't count.

She just carried on trundling the pram back and forth, adding bit by bit to the pile – two or three slabs of stone at a time – and as the pile began to grow, Gourlay's paranoia mounted.

He had only pointed out the fence belonged to her so that she would know. It was only right she should know what was hers, her responsibilities and so forth. The posts were on his side, which meant maintenance was up to her. That was the general rule with fences, and it was fair enough, after all, because she got the better side facing her way. But maybe that's what had got her started.

She must have thought he was complaining about the condition of the fence because it wasn't long after that the stones began to appear. It was small amounts at first. Every day, she pushed the pram up to the field and came back down with a couple of slabs. But, gradually, she began to step up her activities and the loads got heavier. She was making five or six trips, sometimes double, until the wall began to take over – not just her life but Gourlay's as well. He had counted every load as if it was missiles she was stockpiling behind the fence.

When he went out again, the girl was digging up a line of turf on the boundary between the two gardens. It was heavy, slow-going work. After a while, she straightened up and said hello. Gourlay didn't return her greeting. He looked right past her at the piles of stone instead. 'You're not going to make much of a job in this weather,' he said.

'Why's that, then?'

'Subsidence,' he said flatly. Her wall was going to sink. He looked at her square on and smirked. 'The soil's too damp.'

'You think so?' the girl said. She dug her heel into the earth and stared intently at the ground. Then she leaned over and brought her weight down on the spade.

'Now take that wall over there,' Gourlay said, jerking his thumb towards a low wall behind him. 'That was done right. She wanted a raised bed for her alpines,' he explained. 'Not much to look at if you ask me. I prefer roses myself, but it's what she likes.' The girl didn't look too interested in his wall. She stabbed into the ground and jarred the spade against a buried stone.

Gourlay raised his face up the the sky. 'Aye,' he said with some satisfaction. 'It looks like rain.' The girl glanced up balefully and a single drop of rain spat in her eye. Gourlay's lips twitched. The elements were on his side.

The two of them locked in a wordless tussle. The girl flung the spade aside and began to stamp down the earth – short, violent stamps which seemed less directed at the ground than at him. Gourlay folded his arms and watched while he waited for rain and vindication. He knew about things she didn't begin to understand. The weather, for instance. How to build a wall. How to wait. Something that simple.

Gourlay knew how to wait. He'd made a career out of waiting – twenty-five years as a traffic warden. And, over that time, he'd perfected the art of standing about, minimising the amount of exertion necessary to maintain the upright position. He didn't slouch or stand too straight or shift his weight from one foot to another. He didn't even tighten his jaw.

When he stood he just relaxed into it and became completely immobile, except for his eyes, which flickered occasionally over the girl. She was on the skinny side. Hair pulled back from her face and a shapeless black sweater that came down almost to her knees. She had freckled skin and small pale-green eyes, which creased up whenever she spoke. So she would look or speak but not both together. Not that she did much of either. She ignored him most of the time.

Gourlay had come across some stuck-up bitches in his professional capacity. He always gave the snooty ones a ticket. But some of the others. You would be surprised. Some fine-looking women park on double yellow lines. He smiled to himself and looked at the girl side on.

'The woman before you,' he said. He paused for a moment to remind himself of the voluptuous widow in her early forties who had been the previous tenant. The woman before her had been something to look at. Big. Plump. Blooming. Gourlay's taste in women had a lot in common with his taste in flowers. He liked them a bit showy.

'She wasn't interested in the garden,' Gourlay said. 'She wasn't lazy, though. Always working. Busy, busy. Couldn't stop. I think it was some kind of compulsion, but it was decorating with her.' Gourlay frowned and looked thoughtful for a second. 'I think it has something to do with that house,' he said. 'Seems to make folk restless.' The girl raised her eyebrows and carried on stamping. Gourlay cocked his head to one side. 'What are you doing that for?' he inquired.

She didn't answer. She slapped the first stone down between them. 'You could be doing with a hand,' Gourlay said.

She slapped down another stone. 'Are you offering?'

'Tsk. I wasn't meaning myself.' Gourlay was genuinely surprised. He'd been thinking more about one of the men he sometimes saw round at her place. 'Maybe one of your fellas would give you a hand if you asked nicely.'

The girl looked up sharply. 'Maybe I don't want to ask anyone nicely.' She had the missile ready in her hand – a small wedge-shaped lump of stone. She took a step back and weighed it up in both hands for a moment as though she couldn't decide what to do with it. In the end, she let it drop. She bent forward, tugged at the hem of her sweater and began to peel it slowly up over her head. He caught a glimpse of white midriff and soft pink undergarment riding up over angular ribs. The girl let the sweater fall where she stood and tucked the pink vest into the waist band of her jeans. The colour seemed to warm and soften her. Her eyes glowed. Her pale skin took on a subtle lustre. But Gourlay barely noticed any of this. He was transfixed by the outline of small hard breasts beneath the flimsy stretched material.

He thrust his hand deeper into his pockets. The girl was watching him. She'd hardly given him a straight look since she moved in. Her eyes always strayed off to one side or glanced by him. But now she was looking right at him – her pale little eyes wide with contempt. 'Looks like you were wrong about the rain,' she said.

Gourlay didn't answer. He sucked up the saliva behind his teeth and allowed his gaze to return to her breasts before taking aim. Not much there to look at. He spat directly on to the stone she had just laid, then turned back to the house.

In the kitchen, he pulled down the blind. The bitch was kidding herself if she thought he had any interest in her whatsoever. She was nothing special. Line her up with half a dozen parking violations picked at random off the street and he wouldn't give her a second glance. She wouldn't even merit the time it took to write out a ticket.

He poured himself a cup of tea from the pot his wife had left on the stove and sat down at the table. The tea was black and bitter. He heard the boy come back from school. Their voices murmuring together for a moment. A ripple of laughter from the girl and then a shout. GET DOWN. A short tense silence followed before the boy began to roar and Gourlay's wife came bustling into the kitchen. 'What are you sitting through here in the dark for?' She yanked up the blind to see what all the noise was about. 'Would you look at that,' she said.

The boy was lying flat on his back, flailing his arms and legs and yelling fit to bust. The girl was laughing. She grabbed him by the ankles and began to work his legs back and forth like pistons. The boy yelled louder. 'I know what I would do with him,' his wife said.

'Sure you do,' Gourlay replied. He got up and left the room.

Gourlay spent the rest of the evening slumped in front of the television set. His wife appeared at regular intervals with mugs of tea and updates on the girl's progress with the wall. She was still out there at the back of nine. At ten o'clock, his wife popped her head around the door to say that she was off to bed and that the girl had gone in for the night.

Gourlay sat on in the gathering gloom listening to the creaking overhead as his wife prepared for bed. And long after she had settled, he was still sitting there – absolutely motionless. His mind motionless also – except for one slow growing thought. The girl had humiliated him. He wasn't exactly sure how she'd done it, but he knew all the same. He knew. Even in the dark, with nobody to observe him, his heart raced and he flushed at the thought. He got up and went through to the kitchen.

Her light was still on. It illuminated the length of her garden and the bottom corner of his own. The low, ragged outline of the wall ranged between them. It wasn't done yet. She would be out again tomorrow.

The girl came into the kitchen and stopped directly below the light. Her face was white and intense. He could see her through the window very clearly. The pink vest. The black sweater slung across her shoulders. She'd let down her hair and it seemed to float about her head in a pale almost transparent cloud. She stood there a long time, staring out at the wall, apparently unaware that he was watching.

Then, suddenly, her gaze shifted to Gourlay's darkened window. Her lips twisted to one side and her eyes appeared to fix on him. Gourlay ducked as though he'd been caught in the glare of a searchlight and banged his elbow on the table.

75

When he came up again he saw the girl smiling – a secret, satisfied smile – as she turned and walked out of view. The wall was there between them now and that was what she wanted.

The House of Nostalgia

I t was a child's idea of a castle. Not the fairy-tale version. Delicate turrets. Pinnacles rising into an azure sky. More like a sandcastle. Walls muddied by the rain.

Mike had wanted her to race, once round the ramparts and back to the car. And she had started trotting before it crossed her mind to ask what she was doing running after him.

Fiona let him go, leaned back against the hulking wall. For a moment, her eyes closed. But it was not so easy to blot the last five minutes out. Rough stone dug through her leather jacket, reminding her of where she was and how it felt to be on the outside. The visitors had looked so grim. He should've warned her. But no – he'd let her walk right up and join the queue. And she was almost in before she saw the sign above the door. **HM Prison Lancaster.** His idea of a joke.

Fiona was also a visitor today. Last night, she'd taken the train down from Edinburgh to see him. Not that Mike ever did time. Just wasted it – playing Nintendo with his mates while she waitressed split-shifts to support them. For years, his life had been one long lie-in but he was a reformed character these days.

Maybe his thirtieth birthday had something to do with it – middle age rearing its worried head on the not-so-distant horizon. Or maybe all her nagging finally got through. He went on an IT course, then came down here to a job in system support. He owned five ties now, a different one for each day, Monday through to Friday. He was talking about a mortgage, doing everything she'd always said she wanted. She wasn't sure she'd meant it now – that was the thing. She wasn't sure at all.

Fiona turned up her jacket and started back the way she came, arriving at the car just behind him. He was still puffing. Huffing too. Because she had abandoned the race. He wanted to do everything fast these days, drove too fast, couldn't understand why she wasn't rushing down here after him. It made her nervous. This afternoon, she'd tried to tell him she needed time to catch up.

But he just said, 'You're never satisfied.'

And he wouldn't say where they were heading now. There was something he wanted to show her – that's all. 'No kidding, this time,' Fiona said.

'No kidding,' he assured her.

She smiled. The coast was just a few miles away. He knew how much she loved the sea and maybe, if the tide was out, they could build a castle. The beach would be deserted at this time of year. The sea would not be blue. It would be grey like the sky. And they could stand arm in arm, try to make out where one left off and the other began. Sea and sky. Sky and sea. They used to be like that back in the old days, used to blend so easily together.

He turned off the main road and bumped the car down a long rutted track. This was it. The surprise. A building site. A fleet of half-built houses sinking in a field of mud. He said the show house would be open soon.

'So what do you think?'

Fiona rolled down the window and gazed into a ditch. 'An English man's home,' she said.

'What?'

She shook her head. The ditch reminded her of a moat, that was all. Mike snorted and started up the car. Never satisfied. On the way back, he accused her again. He dropped her off in the town centre. It was still raining but she needed to get out and walk. She took shelter in a department store and looked at all the stuff they still couldn't afford. Never satisfied. Maybe he was right. But sometimes it was easier when you didn't have a choice. Easier just to stay where you were. It crossed her mind to head back to the station and call when she got into Waverley.

The northern rain was battering down when she emerged from the store. She ducked her head against the deluge and plunged along the road. Dodging puddles. Eyes fixed on the pavement. So she noticed right away this time. Another sign. A painted board propped against the wall at the entrance to an alley.

To The House Of Nostalgia. The glow from a window beckoned her down. It was a second-hand emporium. Books, clothes, bric-a-brac. The good stuff mixed in with the crap. Fiona wandered round, picking things up as they caught her eye. A pumpkin bowl. A set of three blue china elephants – papa, mama and baby-sized.

She riffled through a rail of clothes, pulling out midnight velvet. A corset-pink slither of silk. A twenties' dress. Silver beaded. Heavy. She weighed it and let it go. The dress swung rattling back on the rack. Even after it had settled, a musty perfume lingered on, hinting at the woman who'd worn it, some bright young thing with shingled hair swaying in the arms of a lover.

She used to dance with Mike back in the old days. They'd come home, tired and stoned, and she would persuade him. Nothing smoochy though. They'd copied it from an old movie – a wild swooping barn dance that climaxed with the guy swinging the gal high up in the air, then down through his legs and her yelling, OKLAHOMAH GOODBYee!

They'd do it till they both fell over laughing and rolling about on the floor. Back then, she'd only been marginally more responsible than him, just enough to keep things ticking.

Since he left to come down here, Fiona had been waking too early in the morning, an hour or more before the alarm, his absence gradually dawning as she surfaced to consciousness. She missed him most before she got going, missed the old warmth.

She had already made up her mind to take the elephants when she found the sampler stuffed in among some books. The glass was cracked, the canvas badly stained.

xxxxxxxxxxxxxxxxxxxxxxxxxxxxxx
HOME is WHERE the HEART is
xxxxxxxxxxxxxxxxxxxxxxxxxxxxxx

The criss-crossed homily was punctuated at the end with a faded brownish-red heart, not so much the colour of passion as shabby familiarity.

The woman behind the counter raised her eyebrows when she saw it. 'Are you sure?' she said. 'It won't clean up, you know.' She wrapped up the elephants one by one and popped them in a carrier, but she seemed reluctant to let the sampler go.

'I don't know what you want it for.'

The woman frowned and Fiona found herself explaining that she was thinking of settling down. It seemed to be the right answer. For, suddenly, the woman beamed a broad, approving smile. 'Tell you what – seeing as you're taking these, I'll fling it in for fifty pee.'

Fiona thanked her. It was getting dark ouside. Mike would be wondering where she'd got to. She slipped the package inside her jacket and headed for the door.

'Good luck,' the woman called out after her.

Fiona waved. Her heart thudded against the sampler as she ran back up the alley. Home is where the heart is . . . home is here . . . here . . . here . . .

The Witch

L eslie Brown is panting and wheezing with excitement. She knows the answer. *Please, miss, please, miss. I know.* She would. All around me, frantic fingers are clicking to be picked. But The Witch has a long nose. She can smell a slacker a mile off. She ferrets them out with her beady eyes and pokes them with sarcasm till they squirm.

The Witch has seen me with my hand down. Her X-ray vision parts the sea of hands and homes in on me. Her eyes bulge. The eyeballs are a sickly, jaundiced yellow. She wants me to tell her the answer. But I don't know.

Well, work it out then.

I still don't know.

Make an attempt.

Um . . .

Wrong, wrong, wrong. I don't know – is incorrect. Big mistake. The answer is – I don't care. Right. Correct. I don't care. There are better questions anyway.

Take, for instance, the square root of The Witch. Now there's a question. She doesn't have red blood. Her skin's so yellow the blood is probably all bilious and black. Probably her organs are all black too. Because her blood is like thick, black treacle. So it sticks to her guts. And the black blood shows through the white skin sort of greenish-yellow and makes her look sea-sick and mean.

The Witch is watching me. She's got bushy black eyebrows that meet in the middle and teeth like the yellowed ivories on an old piano. She's also got a gold filling at the side which you only see when she smiles. And she only ever smiles when she's being sarcastic.

Her eyes are bulging again. Aha – caught one with her hand down. She says she's had enough of my indolence. Put in brackets (A for Apathy + B for Boredom) = C me after class.

So I get extra calculus. The Witch says that, sooner or later, I will understand that mathematics trains the mind. She says that, no matter how diabolical the calculation, there is an answer to every problem. And life isn't meant to be easy, young lady.

The Witch says if I put my mind to it I could get an A. The trouble is my mind refuses to be put to it. As soon as I set foot in her class, it slips sideways and wanders off. She says if I really tried I could do well. Her eyes are a bit watery today. And she has a queer, close-lipped smile. I think there's a bit of The Witch that hurts easy. Or else she's got a head cold. Maybe she's going to sneeze.

She doesn't.

Well, I have to say I'll try. The trouble with maths is you

can't argue with it. All those small, orderly steps. Those absolutely perfect answers. You can't say 99 might make a more interesting answer than 100. You can't say that due to Euclid's limited social environment he could have been mistaken about the shortest distance between two points. Maybe it's not always a straight line. Maybe somewhere else it's curved. I've to hand in the calculus tomorrow. I think she's forgotten there's no class tomorrow.

Hairy legs.

The Witch has hairy shins and black, knotted veins on her calves. I can't understand why she doesn't depilate. What is the point in wearing sheer stockings? The nylon only flattens the hairs and makes them splay. Or they poke through the micromesh. If she was a blonde it wouldn't matter so much.

When I was thirteen, my mum bought me one of those depilatory creams which leaves your legs silky smooth and smells revolting. Gran said she shouldn't pander to my vanity. She says I spend too much time in front of the mirror as it is. Mum said it wouldn't matter so much if I was blonde. But girls of my age are sensitive. And even Caroline, who's Close Brethren and doesn't have a television, bleaches the hair on her legs. Caroline has shiny black hair like mine.

Mum didn't want me to come home crying because of Edward and the Fatboy again.

Edward has a suppurating, acne-pitted nose. And the Fatboy's got piggy eyes and green teeth. So why should I care about their comments? We used to make comments all the time. And they stuck chewing gum in my hair and I pulled theirs. It was just a laugh really. I never mentioned Edward's nose or the Fatboy's teeth. So why did they have to go and make comments about my hairy legs. Girls are not supposed to have hairy legs.

I hope the Fatboy gets so fat he'll never be able to sit with his knees together again. I hope Edward's nose explodes.

The Witch doesn't forget. As there's no class tomorrow I've to hand in the extra work first thing in the morning. Tomorrow is the end of winter term. We'll go to church and sing 'There is a Green Hill Far Away'. The Witch will be wearing face powder and lipstick. She always does on special occasions like end of term assemblies and the senior dance. She paints her mouth true red like a forties movie star. It doesn't suit her. Her lips are too thin and the colour bleeds from the corners of her mouth.

The Witch will look gruesome and happy. She always does at these Events. With the make-up on, her face relaxes. And people snigger. I don't. I wish she wouldn't try. I wish she would go and wipe it off this instant!

I wonder what she was like when she was young. Not pretty. But maybe quite striking. Her figure's still good. Full busted. Slim hipped. I wouldn't mind being that shape. I wonder what she was like when her flesh was fresh and plumped out.

I can see her on an old, black Raleigh cycling to meet her lover. Her black hair curled and bouncing. Blood-red lips. And ivory skinned – I don't think The Witch ever had much colour. Maybe she plucked her eyebrows then. And dyed her legs with tea leaves. She's wearing a gored, knee-length tweed skirt and a simple, boxy blouse.

Her lover is home on leave from World War II and this is the last time she'll ever meet him. No, he didn't die in battle. That's too corny. Grief didn't turn her so sour. No. Maybe, that last night, he gave her a present. A small diamond solitaire which had cost him the best part of three months' pay. She was overjoyed. She couldn't wait for the war to be over. She wrote to him every day.

He also gave her a dose of gonorrhoea which he'd picked up cheap in the desert and she didn't discover till ten months later. She was left infertile and without a good excuse to stop teaching maths to a bunch of snotty kids like me.

Or maybe it wasn't that at all. Maybe during the Allied Advance he met a Roman waitress who shaved her legs and didn't know the perfect answer to everything. He brought her back to his home town and they opened an ice-cream parlour and had four sons. The Witch taught them maths at the local high school and all four of them were hopelessly innumerate but handsome in an Italian-waiter sort of way.

I could stay home tomorrow. It's the end of term. And The Witch might forget about the calculus.

Long Grass, Moon City

R ose lay in the long grass, watching a big, fat cumulus cloud slowly change shape. The grass was bleached yellow but not yet brittle. It must be three feet high. No – that wasn't right. She was exaggerating. More like two. Up to her knees, anyway. High enough for her to lie there and not be seen by anyone passing by. Rose felt ripe and perfectly content.

James was tugging at her arm but she didn't feel like moving right now. He tugged a bit harder. Then, suddenly, toppled backwards and landed comfortably on his bottom. He looked surprised. Rose grinned. She reached over for her bag and pulled out a packet of rusks. That should keep him quiet for a while. She closed her eyes and drifted off, trying not to fall asleep and spoil the sensation of being in between. She got about twenty minutes before the sound of a radio spoiled her peace. Someone was coming her way. She sighed and opened her eyes. James was still sitting in the same spot with the soggy rusk dribbling down his T-shirt. She'd have to change him now.

There were three of them. When Rose sat up they looked over. They were about thirteen – maybe fourteen. One of them had black hair with a bit of a wave in it. He looked over at her again. Rose turned her back and began sponging James's face and hands.

'Hey, missis.' The one with the black hair was coming towards her. He looked like a cocky wee bastard – all strut and snigger. 'Huv ye got a light, missis?'

Rose gave him a dirty look. The missis annoyed her. She said, 'Are you not a wee bit young to be smoking, sonny?'

The boy flushed. 'Don't call me sonny.'

'Well, don't you call me missis, then. Okay?'

The boy stared at her. Rose gave him her matches and he went back to his mates. She turned her back on them and began to change James. She peeled off his T-shirt. Missis. Cheeky wee sod. She could be his big sister. She wasn't even twenty yet. She took a clean top out of the bag and looked down at her swollen belly. Not twenty yet and six months gone again. She pulled the clean top roughly over James's head. Soon as you have a baby you're automatically written off as a missis as far as they were concerned. And what was a missis?

She turned to get the talcum powder and saw that the boys were moving off. 'Hey, you. I want my matches back.'

The boy came back and dropped the matches at her feet. She took a dozen or so out and handed them to him. 'Here. You can have these.' The boy said ta. Neither of them smiled.

She watched the boys cross the burn and cut through a gap

in the high wire fence. They disappeared into the waste ground behind the scheme, where phase three lay abandoned. Before the foundations had even been finished, the blocks in phase one and two were already showing signs of dampness. So phase three had been cancelled and those families in the existing blocks were left to rot – or get out if they could. It wasn't easy to get out.

She lay down and shut her eyes again but it was too late. The boys had spoilt it. If they hadn't come along she might have sung something like – Gershwin. *Summer time and the living is easy. So hush pretty baby* – slow and soulful. Maybe she could get the mood back. She tried humming it quietly to herself but it didn't work. Her voice wavered. Pathetic, she thought. She wouldn't want anyone to come by and catch her singing like that. When you were a kid, you could sing any way you wanted – anywhere you wanted. But she was a mother now.

Sometimes when it rained, she pushed the pram up to Rouken Glen. There was a waterfall there, right at the back behind the woods, and when it had been raining for a few days, it got really noisy and she would lean over the wooden fence, let the spray wet her face and sing anything that came into her head as loud as she wanted.

When Rose got back, Gordon was out on the deck-access, leaning against the parapet. He must have forgotten his keys. A group of women smiled and said hello to her as she passed. It was nice the way the sun brought people out of doors – even though the kids made such a racket, trundling up and down on their bikes.

'Hello. You're early.'

Gordon didn't look at her. He said, 'It's Friday.' Gordon didn't look at her much now – not since she got pregnant again. It was ironic really. There she was getting bigger and bigger and more and more invisible as far as he was concerned.

She gave James to his father and hunted through her bag for the keys. 'Don't tell me you've lost them again. Here, let me have a look.' He put out a hand to take the bag. He was always in such a hurry. She pulled it back from him and went over to the parapet where the light was better and searched through the bag methodically. They were right at the bottom under the polythene bag with the dirty clothes. She handed over the keys and they went inside. 'What kind of day did you have, then?' Rose asked.

'The usual.'

'Oh.' Rose was disappointed. Just for once she wished he would pretend to be happy. He put James down to crawl on the carpet and drew his pay packet out of his back pocket. He put it up on the shelf. Rose looked at it. It had been opened. 'Don't worry,' he said. 'I only took my fare home.'

'I wasn't worried,' she said quietly.

'The rest of them were going to the pub.'

'Why didn't you go too?' As soon as she asked, Rose realised it was a mistake. Had he not made it clear enough to her already? He didn't want to fit in, didn't care what his work-mates made of him. Now he said, 'It's bad enough having to work with that shower of animals all day without going drinking with them when I've finished.'

He was shouting. Rose said she would go and make the

dinner. She lifted James and went through to the kitchen, shutting the door behind her. She stayed there until the food was ready, though all she had to do was switch on the oven. The meal had been prepared earlier. This was one of her organised days. The washing and ironing was up to date. The flat was clean. Everything was in its place and she was in control. This was how it was supposed to be. But it didn't matter what she did, she couldn't make it right for him. When she got pregnant with James, they were both still in college. He was studying photography. He had a good eye, saw things most other folk ignored. He taught her to see them too and she had fallen in love with him, with the way the light fell on a slate roof top, with the deep shadow in the stair well. It was his decision to quit. She'd tried to talk him out of it.

After James, she'd gone back and got her diploma. As soon as this baby was born, she'd be straight out to work. Okay, it wasn't quite what they'd planned. But they would get by. If they could hang on just a few more months . . . she kept trying to tell him. But he had the idea a man should provide, dropped out with one semester to go.

Short-sighted – she told him – when he was so close. And who said they had to give up on their dreams, anyway? There was no law. But he wouldn't listen. And the burden he refused to share was crushing the boy in him, the boy she had loved.

They spent the evening watching television. At 9.30, he switched over. There was a programme about submarines he wanted to see. Rose sighed and lit up a cigarette. 'I thought you'd stopped,' Gordon said.

'I'm bored.' She took a long drag and exhaled slowly through her nose.

He kept his eyes on the screen. 'Do something then.'

'I'm too tired.'

He got up and turned the volume down a bit. 'Where were you today, then?' Rose looked across a him. He was still glued to the submarine programme.

'We went over the back,' she said. 'By the burn. It's lovely over there, almost like being out in the country.'

For the first time that evening, Gordon turned to face her. 'Sometimes, I think you actually like living here,' he said. It was an accusation. He leaned forward. The veins in his neck were standing out. So she knew he was angry.

Rose said quickly, 'It's not that. It's just that where you are – where we are – isn't the only thing. I mean, what we are – that counts for something too. That's more important in the end, isn't it?'

But Gordon didn't have time for existential questions like – who am I? As far as he was concerned, who you were wasn't the problem when you were where they were. 'Look,' he said. 'Listen to me.' He knelt down before her and cupped her face in his hands. She got the feeling he was looking for forgiveness. He was so near she could feel his breath on her eyelids. He couldn't go on he said. It was the job. It was this place. He couldn't hack either. There were things he needed to do. Maybe he would go back to college. But he couldn't do it here. So now he'd said it. He was leaving. Rose began to cry.

She went for a bath. It wasn't all her fault, was it? A year, maybe two years, of hard work and we'll be out of here. That's what they'd said. But the panic set in fast. Before the carpets were even laid, they were wondering if they'd make it back out again. The walls were newly plastered. So they had to wait six months before they could decorate and then they didn't bother because, as Gordon said, that would be like accepting they belonged here and this rat hole was marked. You looked in the mirror and saw the place stamped all over your face. All the same, she would quite like to paint the walls. With a bit of imagination she could transform this place. Then, when they came in and shut the door, they might be able to forget about where they were.

The bath must have revived her. At two in the morning, Rose was restless. Even with the window open and just a sheet to cover her, it was too hot. Gordon was lying diagonally across the bed with one arm dangling over the side. He looked so peaceful now.

She got up, slipped on a robe and a pair of sandals and went out to the hall. The key was in the door. Rose unlocked it and stepped out. The scheme looked like moon city at night. All those semi-circles of light on the deck-access and fragile bridges in the sky, linking one crescent block to another. She felt like she was in a big, plastic bubble. The air smelt sharp and clean but fresh air wasn't natural in this artificial landscape. At night, it was easy to imagine she was inside some man-made dome with manufactured air and expensively imported damp-earth smells.

Sometimes, on a good night, Gordon could almost be persuaded to see the scheme her way for a change. A pair of aliens – that's what they were. She'd make it sound like an adventure. But in the uncompromising light of day he saw it with his camera-clear eye, couldn't or wouldn't alter his focus, blur the hard edges, tint grey concrete with hope – the way she did.

Your daddy's rich and your mama's good lookin'. So hush . . . Rose was humming as she walked along to the end of the block. She couldn't decide whether to go downstairs or cross the spindly bridge to the next block. It was possible to get from one end of the scheme to the other without going down to ground level. She stopped and leaned over the parapet. There was only so much that could be done to create an earth-like environment. The trees hadn't taken root too well up here. They looked gawky and out of place. Nothing was quite as it should be. All the same, she felt safe here. It was a self-contained, little colony and it was hard to imagine what lay outside.

She heard footsteps behind her. A man she knew vaguely by sight, stopped at the top of the stairs to catch his breath. 'Bloody inhuman, hen – these stairs. You realise if this building had been one storey higher they would've had to give us a lift?' Rose nodded politely. He came over and leaned on the parapet next to her. He smelled of beer and perspiration.

'You ever seen the scale model of what this place is supposed to look like?'

Rose shook her head. 'No – but I've heard about it.' The original plans were often referred to like rumours of paradise.

'All lies,' the man said. 'They never had the budget. Never had any intentions. I was a brickie. Worked right here on the site. Didnae think I would end up here, though.' The man smiled grimly. In the moonlight, his face shone with sweat. 'So if you get the chance, hen, see if you get the chance to get out of here, don't waste it. This is no place to bring up a family. Christ knows, you don't have to look too far to see how this place is going.'

They both looked down at the refuse scattered around the bin area. The communal waste-disposal chute was blocked again. And someone clearly couldn't be bothered to make the trip downstairs. So far it hadn't started an avalanche but Rose could sense it coming soon, the balance tipping from order to chaos. She closed her eyes.

It was a million miles back to earth and if she was ever going to get there, she'd have to make the journey alone.

An Immaculate New Year

All Goldie wanted was to sink back to sleep and forget. But the mattress refused to give way. It told her very firmly that this was not her bed. She was trespassing.

Last night, lit by the waxing moon, the room had been a deep, dark, velvet blue and he had led her by the hand. This morning, it was still blue. But faded now. Curtains of muted lavender silk. Walls the shade of a pale sky. A subtle room. The woman it belonged to would notice the little things, spot the clue in a newly smoothed quilt, would know at a glance someone had been visiting.

Where was his wife now?

'Somewhere a lot warmer than this,' he'd said bitterly, after the bells last night. 'The Seychelles.'

He drew Goldie down in front of the fire. They'd lain on the hearth rug, heart of the home, with Christmas cards to him and his wife, coal-eyed snowmen and twinkly Santas smiling down from the mantelpiece, best wishes from friends and family.

They hadn't met Goldie. They wouldn't want to. But their cards had given her such a warm feeling, she didn't care if it was stolen. Last night, she'd basked in the glow of their greetings.

Goldie didn't get any cards of her own. You needed an address to get mail, your own door, a letterbox, your own special key. She could hear him down below now, the vacuum-cleaner going on. She'd spilt ash on the carpet. She was a slob that way. 'Sloppy slut,' he said last night when she missed the ashtray. His tongue had licked around the words, slid between her smoky lips.

Goldie pulled the quilt up round her ears to shut out the noise. He'd better not be hinting she should be up and dressed. It was annoying when they did that. She was a visitor, after all. But, sometimes in the morning, they forgot their manners. They didn't want to wake up next to the proof of their loneliness, didn't want to remember how they'd needed her to listen.

His wife didn't cook. Never ironed his shirts. And she just dropped her tights and knickers where she stood. He was always picking up after her. But she used to need him.

'Not like you,' he said last night. His long face sagged.

His wife had faxed him at the office, faxed him where it hurt the most. She wanted a clean break, wished him a spotless Christmas and immaculate New Year.

His wife had wanted a child. They both had – he said. But they had never really tried. They'd forgotten time was passing and then it was too late.

Goldie had sympathised. She understood about forgetting.

Things slipped her mind all the time. Some people called it thoughtlessness. But that was their opinion. She liked that clean empty feeling of nothing in her head.

When she moved on, she would forget him. His tired eyes. His sad long face. He was old enough to be her father, just about. She could be his.

When she was eight or maybe nine, she used to dream of stealing her friend Tracy's dad. She'd sneak into Tracy's house, put on Tracy's brown-suede pinafore and her orange polo top, tie up her hair with Tracy's ribbon. Tracy's hair was honey blonde and hers was honey gold but no-one seemed to see the difference. They got them mixed up all the time.

She'd slip on Tracy's new best shoes. And when her dad got in from work, he would call her sweetheart and lift her high and whirl her round just like he always did. And she would shriek and laugh her head off because she was his. His sweetheart. His cuckoo in the nest.

Goldie could belong to anyone. Anyone she visited.

She could hear him down below now, glasses clinking in the sink. He'd picked her clothes up off the floor, hung the jade silk shirt behind the door. It was only ten to seven according to the bedside clock. Maybe all this up-and-busy had something to do with his resolution. Last night, he'd said they both should make one.

And she had said – what for?

His wife had no sense of humour. 'Not like you,' he'd said. 'You don't take me seriously, do you?'

Ah, but maybe she would like to.

Today, the new year stretched ahead so far she couldn't see

the end. How many visits would she pay? How much more could she forget? Goldie rolled over to the edge of the bed and hugged her knees up to her chest.

She used to stay with Gran sometimes, when her mum couldn't cope. One time, she'd stayed for months on end. But she was only visiting. She couldn't stay for ever. Gran said it wouldn't be right.

Her gran was always nagging. Pick up your plate. Put on your scarf. Just about throttled her, she pulled it so tight. But Goldie didn't mind. She got porridge every morning and sausages on Sundays. And the curtains were all shades of yellow, so even on the dullest day the light came through like sunshine.

She dreaded the return to gloom. The heavy atmosphere – laced with cigarette smoke, soured with sherry dregs. The thick lined velour curtains – always drawn too soon, holding in the tension, shutting out the world.

Last night, she said, 'Don't close them.'

He didn't seem to mind.

Goldie smiled at the teddy bear propped up on the window-sill. It was the old-fashioned kind with movable arms and legs. Tawny glass eyes. A leather snout. Patchy matted fur. Bare bits where the comfort had been all hugged out.

The bear belonged to his wife. He'd mentioned it last night. He said it meant a lot to her, worth a bit of money too, and he was sure she would be back. She wouldn't leave her precious bear.

A shaft of winter sunlight trained on a worn strip in the carpet, revealing traces of the path he and his wife had worn between them. It was a cool room with all the blues. But his wife was somewhere warmer now. She wouldn't need the teddy where she was. Goldie gazed into the bear's brown eyes. The warm expression didn't change. She always took a little thing to pawn when it was time to move on. But this was something she might take to keep. Something she could hold on to.

She squinted up at the blouse again. It was remarkably uncrushed considering. Not a wrinkle. Not a crease. She wondered if he had been ironing. Some places seemed okay at first and then you noticed something. Maybe in the bathroom cabinet. She always checked in there. Maybe just a little thing in a careless place. Then it was time to leave.

But there was nothing here. None of the grubby signs of living – eating, shitting, shedding skin. Not a thing out of place except her. Everything so perfect – he just had to be weird. Goldie stumbled out of bed and slid into her clothes, gasping as her skin shrunk from the icy silk shirt.

He came in with a bundle of fresh linen. 'So who's been sleeping in my bed?' he said.

She watched him pull back the quilt. His head cocked critically to one side. His mouth pursed. And in his eyes – a quick gleam of interest as they lit upon a golden hair. A pubic curl. He leaned over and examined it more closely, sniffed the air. His nose flared. Then he drew back. He gathered up the soiled sheet, smiling grimly to himself.

'So how do you take your porridge?' he asked.

Goldie didn't answer.

She could take it salt. She could take it sweet. But it could never be just right. Not here. She clutched the bear tight as she skipped downstairs and out through the front door – skated down the frozen path into an immaculate new year.

Lying Still

O utside room 16, a skinny red-haired boy was peering through a narrow pane of glass in the door. He was waiting for the right moment to knock and enter. Cassidy wasn't going to believe his excuse even if it was the truth. He was having trouble believing it himself.

The truth. He was in deep trouble again and he wished he did not have red hair. He wished he was mousey brown and easily over-looked, the type Cassidy might dismiss with a nod. But it was no use hoping for that. And anyway, it was more than the red hair. He wasn't sure what it was but he knew that there was something unforgivable about him.

He ducked into the room. Forgot to knock. Forgot all about getting the timing right. And nobody seemed to notice. Rows of upturned faces fixed on the board, where Mr Cassidy stood with the chalk poised to write. The teacher's mouth was slightly ajar, as if he were about to speak. But he didn't. Not right away. Nobody looked at the boy.

The classroom was so still he could have been walking into a freeze-frame picture. For a minute, he thought his wish had been granted. He was invisible. He could cross the room. Sit down. Give Cassidy the vicky. And the film would roll on.

The boy smiled. For a moment, he forgot he was in trouble. He had an unfortunate face. Pale, close-set eyes, a long nose and prominent chin combined to turn every smile into a sneer or, at best, a smirk. Mr Cassidy roared. 'Miller, stand up straight. Hands out of your pockets.'

The boy felt every muscle in his body contract to the point of physical pain. He pulled back his shoulders and held himself to attention, his head poked forward, arms stuck to his sides. Cassidy had a stiff back and a thick red neck. He was asking why Miller was late, but the boy's tongue had gone big and numb. The words wouldn't come. He went on staring dumbly at Cassidy's neck and tried to swallow. His tongue was choking him.

Cassidy moved away. He went to his desk, unlocked the top drawer and brought out the tawse. For a moment, Miller's eyes went out of focus. Then he shrieked, 'Please, sir, it was ma dad. He couldnae spare me.' The teacher advanced towards the boy, holding the belt out before him in both hands, almost lovingly, as if it was an offering. He knew about Miller's father. The man had a newsagent's and Miller was expected to help out before school. The boy was late every other morning. He knew quite well where Miller had been. Nevertheless dumb insolence could not be ignored. Miller had been given the chance to explain himself, but for some obstinate reason he refused to take it. Therefore, he should hold out his hand.

The teacher explained all this to Miller slowly and carefully. But now Miller's arms were the problem. They were laden down by the weight of his big boney hands. 'Please, sir, it wisnae my fault.'

Cassidy waited for the boy to pull himself together.

At eleven o'clock the place exploded. Seven hundred gabbling voices merged into one huge unified hum, surged through the corridors and out into the playground. Billy McLean nudged Miller. 'You okay?'

'Uhuh.'

Billy had a square muscular body, shaggy fair hair and the sort of cocky self-assurance that is granted only to the chosen few. He didn't mind being seen with Miller.

Sibyl caught up with them in the corridor. 'Poor James,' she said. She was the only one who called Miller by his first name. Miller tried to sidle away from her but Sibyl wouldn't leave him alone. She cornered him again outside. She kept on saying actually. 'Actually, I think Mr Cassidy would be in big trouble if the headmaster found out how often you actually get the strap. I think your mother should complain, actually.'

Actually, Miller wished she would just piss off and leave him alone. Billy McLean was standing behind her making faces. Billy liked Sibyl. 'But Miller doesn't actually have a mother. Isn't that right, James, dear? You don't have a mother, do you?'

Miller frowned.

'See, Sibyl, you've gone and upset the poor boy. You don't have a mother, do you, James?'

Miller shook his head slowly.

'See, Sibyl, it's only posh folk like you that can afford to have mothers. Miller's only got a ma. Isn't that right, James, dear. You've only got a ma?'

Miller sniggered. Billy stared at Sibyl until she began to blush. He just loved the way she ran across the playground to her friends. 'She'll be talking about us,' he said.

He headed for the pitch. Miller followed. 'I wouldnae listen to her if I was you,' Billy said. He took a quick look back to see if Sibyl was still talking about him. 'You're gonnae look a right sissy if your ma comes up to see Cassidy. And you shouldnae let him see you're feart. It makes him worse if he thinks you're feart.'

'Aye, Billy, you're right.'

Billy was never wrong. He was hard, unstoppable as he steam-rollered his way down the pitch and scored. 'Great goal, Billy. Great goal, man,' Miller yelled. Wee Ronnie Sinclair in goal called for offside but nobody paid any attention. Boys from both sides trotted up to slap Billy on the back.

Seconds later, Billy had the ball again, did a neat side step and flicked it back to Miller. Miller floundered, took a left-footed swipe, missed and slithered to his knees. He made a grab for the ball and fell down clutching it to his chest.

'Aw for fucksake, Miller. What are you daein'?'

Miller didn't move. He didn't make a sound. Everyone stared at the tears streaking down his face. Then the bell rang and they turned away.

Miller was left in the middle of the pitch, hugging the scuffed football and thinking of his mother. Not that his ma had ever been much help to him. *Try to look useful when your da's around* was the only advice she ever gave him. But somehow, he never got the hang of looking useful. Miller was used to punishment. He took a lot of stick from the boys at school as well. At least, he used to. That was before he discovered that if he just stood there and let them batter him they went away quicker. It really sickened them when he wouldn't fight back. Now they hardly ever bothered him at all. Just the other day Ronnie Sinclair hadn't battered him.

'You're no supposed to dae that,' he'd said to Sinclair. And Sinclair told him to piss off and went on writing obscenities on the wall. But Miller didn't budge. He wasn't even worried when Sinclair turned to his mates and said, 'Miller's got a heid that was made for kicking.' Miller actually laughed. That was nearly too much but in the end Sinclair only advised him to screw the nut before it came aff.

After the break, Mr Cassidy stood in the doorway, smiling and calling for silence. His lips twitched as he surveyed the class. His eyes lit on Miller's empty desk.

'McLean. Stand up. Where's Miller?'

'Outside, sir.'

'And why is he still outside?'

'Dunno, sir.'

Cassidy frowned. 'Go and get him, McLean. Now.'

Billy found Miller where he'd left him – his gangle of a body spread-eagled on the football pitch. He was spattered with mud and just lying there staring at the sky, his eyes screwed up against the sun.

'You're for it, Miller. Cassidy wants to see you.' Miller didn't answer. He didn't even bother to look at Billy. Billy kicked him gently in the kidneys. 'C'mon. Are you gonnae come quietly or what?'

'Piss off, McLean.' Miller felt vaguely pleased with the level tone of voice he'd used. Usually he was too shrill. And he wasn't going to move. He was just going to lie there for a while and then – maybe later – he would think what to do. One thing he wasn't going to do was go back to Cassidy's class. He would die first. He thought about all the ways he could die. There was death by drowning. Or he could fling himself under a train. They'd know he meant business then.

Or there was pills. But where would he get them? And anyway his dad would probably think pills was a namby-pamby, Nancy-boy way to kill yourself. No. Probably the best thing was to do nothing. He would just lie there and refuse to budge. And what could Cassidy do about that? Nothing. Oh sure, he could get the headmaster. His ma. Maybe even his dad. They would shout no doubt. He could cope with that. All he had to do was lie still.

'Are you coming then?' Billy was circling round him, kicking at tufts of grass and trying to look casual.

'Nope.'

'And what am I supposed to say tae Cassidy?'

'Just tell him – I refuse to move. Okay? I refuse to move.'

Billy wavered for a moment. 'You're off your nut,' he said. He turned to go.

Miller's face was transfigured by a blissful smile. Maybe he was crazy, but what were any of them gonnae do about it.

Pointed Toes

O n the day he finally became dispensable, his wife went out and bought three new pairs of shoes. They pleased her so much that, for almost a week, she couldn't keep her eyes off her feet. She walked lightly, pointing her toes in different directions and standing in experimental poses.

The low, black pumps were cleverly cut at the front to make her feet look a couple of sizes smaller – 4½ or 5 at the most. They were so dainty she felt like a geisha girl. She stood with her toes pointed outwards and considered taking up ballet again. She'd bought the emerald sandals in a sale. Perhaps they were too exotic. She decided to paint her toenails fuschia pink. The effect was outrageous. But the stilettos were the best of all – 3½ inches high, in classic navy. She liked to listen to them click as she walked down the street. It was a very satisfying noise.

The husband admired the shoes, and suggested some new clothes. A dress, perhaps. She should wear more. He made appreciative noises about her shape. This unexpected interest made her edgy. He didn't usually notice what she wore. Then, he infuriated her by apologising for hard times – as though it was his fault he had lost his job. She wished he wouldn't be so nice. She'd just blown a week's pay on the shoes. Why didn't he shout at her? It was unfair of him to take all the blame. She wouldn't let him. He was being greedy – grabbing all the guilt for himself. She would prefer to dispose of the guilt altogether, like her worn-out shoes. The dustbin was the place for lost causes. And, anyway, why should he get the credit for her misery? It was her own.

She said, 'Let's call it quits.' And he knew that she was quitting on more than just hard times.

The wife was pleasant but remote. She had grown to be so comfortably self-contained. Her life revolved around her job, her home, her plants, her books, her friends. She took a dance class twice a week. There was no room for change – no room for him. When he spoke to her she smiled, but her eyes glanced past him to something beyond. She said no more than was necessary and seemed startled when he entered a room, as though she had forgotten he was still there.

Three days a week, the wife went to work. They needed the money now. Without her, the house became unrecognisable. It seemed to him that the furniture, the lamps, the plants, even the crockery had been carefully arranged according to some mysterious plan. Only she knew why. He couldn't relax and spent his days waiting for her to come back. After a while, he began to change a few things round. Nothing much to start with. The first time, he moved the settee to face the fire and placed a low table next to it. Then he put a lamp and some of his books on the table. His wife was late that evening. He put his feet up on the settee and waited for her to return. When she did get home, she said a quick hello and disappeared into the kitchen, refusing his offers of help. She made no comment on the changes.

He couldn't bear the isolation. In an attempt to get her attention, he cranked up old, mechanical arguments and tossed them into the kitchen like grenades. He criticised the food. Was she not aware that saturated fats clogged up the arteries? She offered to make him a salad.

Not only that, saturated fats were politically immoral. Meat production was a waste of resources, a major, cause of food shortages in the third world. He simply could not understand her aversion to brown rice.

She agreed with him. Her dislike of brown rice was irrational. Did he want mayonnaise on his salad?

He examined the label and said he would sooner eat horse shit. She laughed and said, 'Well, at least that's natural.'

He took this as a criticism. She was always telling him not to be so neurotic about what he ate. He accused her of intolerance. She was stupid, he said. Self-satisfied. She wondered why he didn't just accuse her of trying to poison him and be done with it. But, for once, she didn't say it. He said she had no idea what was going on out there in the real world.

She didn't respond. She didn't even slam the door as she went out. This wife, who used to hurl back the most venomous abuse – double tit for tat – had suddenly declared a unilateral truce. Disarmed – he was bewildered.

The wife became vague and forgetful. Sometimes, he caught her staring into space. When he asked what she was thinking she said *nothing much* and looked at him strangely, as if she couldn't figure out what he was doing there. There were such a lot of things she couldn't remember. She couldn't remember what it felt like to be with another man – the adrenaline, the tension, the unfamiliar rhythm and scent. She couldn't remember what it felt like to have a whole bed to herself – the sensation of cool cotton sheets on a hot night, with no-one to stick to and no-one to tell her to turn out the light. And, even more important, she couldn't remember when she had stopped wanting to be with him all the time. She used to resent him going to work. She would drag him back to bed, make him late and spend her days waiting for him to come home again. And now he was there all day, she only felt sorry for him.

It made his wife uncomfortable to see him suddenly slumped. She had relied on this man once. But he was, after all, no stronger than her. Maybe weaker. One thought nagged at her: that she may have sapped his strength and taken it for herself – shades of Samson and Delilah. She felt a heavy pain behind her eyes, but she couldn't cry.

Once, she told him that she found it difficult to believe that he actually worked when he was away from her. It seemed preposterous. All he ever mentioned was the office patter, the coffee breaks and the disruptions. He couldn't believe she was saying this. What did she think a draughtsman did all day? Ten years on the job and she still had no idea what it was like for him. Of course, he hadn't told her about the day in, day out boredom of it all. He hadn't mentioned the fact that every

Sunday night for the past ten years he had considered chucking it in. Oh no – he definitely hadn't told her that. And now he hated her for not knowing.

The winter came and went silently. They moved around each other with caution. Her face said *Do not disturb*. And he didn't try. He was tired. It was a chilling peace, accustomed as they were to the everyday hostilities.

And then one night he nudged her out of feigned sleep. 'Look. Up there – a moving light in the sky. What is it?' He whispered urgently in the dark.

She sat up, rubbing her eyes. 'I can't see anything. Maybe it was a plane. The airport's over in that direction.'

'No. It's still there. Why can't you see it?' She heard the rasp of rising exasperation in his voice and tried to look harder.

'Look.' He put an arm around her shoulder. 'Where my finger's pointing. Can you see it – out there coming in from the stars, red and green and violet lights?'

Ah yes. She could see it now.

'It can't be a star. It's too near.' He whispered in her ear as if he was afraid to disturb the huge forces of space and time. As if the light might stop in its tracks, sensing the naked man and woman, huddled together, eavesdropping on the universe.

They lay awake, one cool skin skimming the surface of the other, and, as they watched, the light appeared to rotate and move towards them. They speculated on what it could be. Perhaps the pulsating lights were some kind of signalling code.

She wished it would come to them quickly. The violet light sent a message of hope. She was sure of that. The green seemed to be growing in power. It throbbed out healing rays. And the red light augured something quite new that couldn't be named or even imagined.

They watched for hours but the light got no closer and they subsided to make love in the cold dawn light. Their bodies seemed nebulous. I could put my hand right through his chest, she thought. He would feel no pain, only the vaguest sensation of bodies floating within bodies, overlapping spaces.

That night, they didn't roll apart to their separate dreams. They rested lightly together, uncovered to the waist. And, as his head grew heavy on her breast, her last thought was that he always spotted the magic first. Maybe she needed him just for that and nothing else.

It was Venus they had seen. The following day, he called her at work just to tell her. He was so enthusiastic it made her want to cry. She turned away from her colleagues and fixed her gaze on her feet. She was wearing the navy stilettos. The heels were a bit rocky now and the toes were scuffed. She thought that nothing – good or bad – lasts for ever, and wondered if they were worth repairing. When her husband finally said goodbye, she put down the phone and went back to work wishing it was five o'clock.

Honey for Later

L ala couldn't handle his kind of living anymore. She knew that the day Terry answered the door without any clothes. She could have been anyone. The postman. A stranger. Shy Mrs Abyanker from across the landing.

He seemed pleased to see her. 'Come in. Come in. You're just in time.'

For what? she wondered. He hadn't been expecting her. She walked past him into the kitchen and sat down at the table, curiously inspecting the congealed remains of a bean stew. Black-eyed and adzuki. The green stuff was probably parsley. He put parsley in everything. And garlic. She sniffed. His kitchen was a good place to be. Today it smelt of nutmeg and lemon-scented tea.

Terry came in behind her, pulling an ancient sweater over his head, and wrapped her into a bear hug. He smelled better than he looked. He hadn't shaved for days. She hoped he wasn't trying to grow a beard because the stubble was red and wouldn't match his hair, but she didn't say so. She said she was cold and he offered to light a fire. He'd made soup with brown lentils, parsley and lots of root vegetables because he'd had a feeling she would come today.

Lala didn't offer to help. She stayed huddled in her coat with the collar turned up to her ears.

'You didn't bring Sandy.'

'No.' Lala could see he was disappointed but she didn't bother to explain. She didn't say anything for a while, just watched the way his backside tightened and relaxed as he moved between the cooker and the work top, held her breath when he put a match to the fire.

He came back to the table with steaming bowls of soup and thick-cut wholemeal bread. There was no butter but he produced an unopened jar of honey.

'For later,' he said.

He left the room. Lala hoped he had gone to put on some decent clothes but he came back in the same old sweater, brandishing a little silver flute. It was a penny whistle, a surprise for Sandy. He wanted her to have a go, play something, but she refused. So he played 'Ally Bally Bee'. She shuddered.

'You should be warmed up by now.'

She pursed her lips.

'Take it with you. Tell Sandy I'll teach her a tune when I see her.'

Lala snapped. 'She's only two for god's sake. She can't blow her own nose yet, never mind anything else.' She glared at him across the table, surprised by her own reaction. What did it matter? Sandy would like it anyway.

'Where is she today, then?' he asked.

'With Mum. She's got the cold.' Without Sandy, there didn't seem much more to say.

He began to sup his soup. Lala stared down into her bowl. It was a thick, dark brew of broth, intended to stick to her ribs. He wanted her fat and comfortable so she couldn't hurt him. Her bones dug at him.

She stirred the soup around the bowl.

He said, 'Eat up.' He always said she was too thin. She talked too much and chewed too little and didn't know what her body needed. He had to remind her Today though, she had nothing to say and no appetite either.

He offered her the honey pot. She shook her head and put the spoon down in the bowl. Maybe she was sickening for the same thing as Sandy. Terry felt her forehead, then got up and cleared all the good things from the table. He was disappointed. He'd made enough soup for six, two times three, in case she brought Sandy and stayed for tea.

Lala made her apologies staring tight-faced at the wall and the peeling paper. She wished she hadn't come today. Without Sandy there to distract her, she noticed things. The hoover had packed in its struggle over two years ago, before Sandy was born, and look how she'd grown. God alone knew what was growing on the carpet. She could visualise Sandy now, crawling across the floor, climbing on top of him, the pair of them laughing and rolling about in the dirt.

'This place could do with a good scrub and a lick of paint,' she said.

He said, 'Move in and we'll do it together.' It sounded causal, but he had never suggested living here before. She waited for him to say something more. But that was it.

And now he was pulling her to her feet. There were some things he could get together. The room next door was ordered and functional. The floor laid with pale new linoleum. The windows bare. One wall was lined with steel frame shelving. Another taken up with banks of keyboards and speakers.

He had something he wanted her to hear. 'One, two. One, two. Love you, Lala.' He smacked a kiss into the mike and waved her to a non-existent chair. The opening arpeggios flew from his hands. His voice swooped and soared around the room. It would be good. He didn't need her to tell him that.

Her attention wandered off the music, down his back to the muscular calves dangling from the stool. He looked daft. Maybe Sandy was young enough to take him the way he was. Lala didn't want to anymore and she was fed up being a visitor.

There was nowhere to sit. She went over to the window. A flock of birds was gathering above the tenements, circling higher and higher. Lala watched them and tried to synchronise their movements to the music. It always amazed her that quite random events could happen together with such perfect timing. Even when the last stragglers had checked in, they stayed on, hovering in the sky, as if they were waiting for a signal to send them south. And, sure enough, they flew away, gradually diminishing to specks on the horizon and disappearing altogether as the music faded out. Lala wanted to hang on to them a bit longer. She screwed up her eyes and strained to catch a final sight. But they were gone.

So what was she still waiting for? Lala wasn't sure but the answer wasn't up there. She needed something definite from him, something more than a casual suggestion.

Back in the kitchen, the timing was not so good. It was half past two. She had to be going. Her mum hadn't been too happy about watching Sandy. But Terry insisted on making her a cup of camomile tea. He wanted to know if they would be coming on Saturday. If it was a good day, they could go for a walk along by the canal. It was frozen over now, thick enough to take his weight. Some of the local kids were skating on it. Sandy would love that.

But Lala couldn't manage Saturday. She didn't know when she would see him next. She was going to be busy looking for a place of her own. They'd been at her mother's far too long.

'You could come here,' he said. He took the cup from her abruptly. The pipe screeched as he turned on the tap to rinse it out.

Lala could see the panic in his eyes. He didn't want her to move on. He didn't want her to stay here. But he was prepared for change – if she pushed.

She shook her head. 'I'd better go.' A glint from the table caught her eye. It was the penny whistle. 'Sandy's going to love this.' She slipped it into her bag.

He called out after her. 'You've missed the bus.'

'Probably,' Lala whispered. She let his door click shut behind her.

The Bridge

B lackmuir – three miles from the motorway, one and a half off the nearest A, down at the bottom of a dead-end road. It is flanked on one side by the river, the railway track on the other. The train doesn't stop. Even the river rushes by on its way to more important destinations.

When Linda arrived, it was in full spate and the roar washed over her, rhythmic and soothing, wiping the memory. She wasn't ready to think back too far, not yet.

Last night, when Duncan began his confession, she'd been half-expecting it. She was prepared, she thought. They'd been together fifteen years and they would probably survive. He said he liked being married to her. She was the only woman. He'd wept and she had held him, watched herself comfort him in the wardrobe mirror.

It was late September and they hadn't turned on the heating yet. It was difficult to feel much below a certain temperature.

She could have done with a sweater. In the morning, she packed and drove up north.

Blackmuir – a huddle of grey stone cottages, a telephone kiosk and the big house. Even the autumn gave the place short shrift. Winter arrived early here and, like an unwelcome guest, always hung around the longest. When his dad was still alive, she'd left it to Duncan to visit through the darkest months. In all those years, nothing much had ever changed here except the seasons.

So the big house was a shock when she first saw it again. No longer blending unobtrusively into the prevailing gloom, it had been painted a vibrant pink.

For the first few days, Linda kept a look-out for the occupant. There was only one – a small, slender man, who scurried from car to door, door to car. He never looked up, never once stopped to gaze at the dying blaze in the trees that edged his garden. He was disappointing somehow, didn't live up to the bold new mood of the big house and she got the feeling he did not belong here any more than her.

Soon, she settled into a routine. The roar of the river woke her in the morning and lulled her back to sleep again at night. In between, she lived a well-regulated life. If it wasn't too cold, she went for a walk, the same route every day, following the river downstream until she reached the wooden bridge.

The river narrowed at this point, thrust its way through a dark gorge. The bridge was rickety, slimed green with algae. And there were gaps where the planks had rotted at the seams, one near the middle – big enough to slip a foot through. She'd tried it once, took a step into the misted air, felt her blood pump, the immediacy of fear. After that, she always stuck near the edge but she still stared, down and down, into the swift wild water, kept on staring until her mind became a perfect blank and everything in her world stopped except the river.

She never met anyone on these excursions, not face to face, though once she'd spotted the man from the pink house on the far side. The bank plunged sharply from his path, almost sheer, and he had walked with studied care, eyes fixed on the muddy track. She'd stopped to watch, held her breath, half-expecting the ground to slide away beneath his feet. Linda felt she could have willed it if she'd wanted. He had looked so unsure, even a malicious thought could have been enough to topple him. She'd turned away before he saw her. But it had been so tempting to push, to breathe out hard and think her worst.

The following day, she drove into the nearest town and bought gallons of white paint. Duncan was supposed to have made a start on the redecorating. In the six months since his dad died, he'd been back often enough. She could have helped. She'd made the offer. They could have got somebody in. But no – he said this was something he needed to do by himself. She'd given him space, waved him off on Saturday mornings to make his peace, lay ghosts to rest. Sometimes, hard labour was the best way. She had been so understanding.

Every day, she painted another wall. The white was clean and blank, a canvas waiting to be brought to life, waiting for a simple shape, a daub of colour to give it meaning.

Every night, she stood at the window and waited for the midnight train. It hurtled by, bound for the south, London, home. The inter-city was a test. She passed if she didn't want to be on it. Every night, she failed and, seconds after the train shot through, an upstairs light in the pink house went out. She often wondered why he waited too, what ritual he went through in the approaching moments.

The weeks passed in silence. She hadn't spoken more than half a dozen sentences all winter. She didn't even think in words anymore. Words were for remembering and planning. The past. The future. Too many memories needed reassessing. She wasn't ready to make decisions yet.

Letters from Duncan lay unopened. The cottage didn't have a phone. She wrote once to let him know where she was and not to come. She wrote again to say she still couldn't tell him how much longer she'd remain in this grey, desolate place.

The cottage was spartan: a stove; rock solid bedstead; and an old oak table with four matching chairs and dresser, which Duncan said was too good for the skip. The rest had gone already.

That winter, Linda began to learn what she needed and what she could do without. She lived out her routine – walking, painting, waiting for the midnight train – until the walls were done, and then, one day out on her walk, she'd passed a small boy on a bike. He ducked his head when she smiled. She was still a stranger here.

There was a rustle in the woods that day too, signs of life stirring below the drifts of mouldering leaves. As Linda approached the bridge, she saw the man from the pink house was already there. Getting close to halfway across, he paused, plunged his hands into his pockets and peered down through the gap. She wondered what he was feeling now. Did his heart skip? Did he sense her willing him to slip, first a foot, then skinny hips?

He stepped over and looked up as she reached her end of the bridge. There was only room for one. But the waiting gave her the advantage somehow. Time to observe. Time to judge. His mouth – a tense, tight line. His gaze – not quite reaching her until he drew almost level. He focused then. Nodded.

It was her turn now. She stepped on to the bridge. She should have nodded back, said hello perhaps. But her lips had frozen and, over the damp dead winter months, her tongue had rusted on its hinges. She couldn't trust it not to creak out some remark of its own choosing.

Linda was almost at the gap before she remembered she had not intended to come this far. Her feet had carried her all the more surely because here head was not involved and now, when she looked down, the river seemed to rise and meet her in a fury of white spume.

It was his chance now. She sensed him watching from the bank, waiting to see if she'd turn back, willing her to test herself against the gap, the hypnotising nothingness. Would she let it suck her in or step across to the beyond? His usual side. Her husband's too, the last few times he'd been out of town. How often had Duncan climbed that treacherous path to the pink house?

She gazed down blindly through the gap, twisting her wedding band round her fourth finger. The owner's name was David. And he was different, Duncan said. Not like the others.

He was certainly different from Duncan. She could see that. So thin. So intense. Her husband was exuberant, a big man in every way. Big voice. Big surface area. And that was where he liked to live, on the surface. Duncan was essentially shallow.

Maybe that was why he'd had to tell her, this time. David was way too deep, dangerous, threatening to drag him in over his head. He'd wanted her to save him.

Linda slipped the band from her finger. It should be easy to let the ring fall into the froth. The trouble was she had been happy married to Duncan. Maybe it had never been the most passionate partnership but it was tender. And it had never been boring.

Duncan, the entertainer, played to a full house of the weekends, dished the dirt on friend and foe along with the pasta.

Duncan the wheeler-dealer, he could sell anything. Ice to the eskimos. Salt to Siberia. 'Sell me too if you got a decent offer,' she'd say to him. And he would look her up and down, sizing the potential, then shake his head. 'You're priceless, sweetie,' he always said.

Maybe their marriage was just another one of his deals with the world, Duncan the survivor. But it had worked.

That night back in the cottage, she stood alone by the window. This was the last time she would wait for the late train. Tonight, she knew she would pass the test. There would be no going back. Tomorrow, she would cross the bridge and take the path to the pink house. She would give David the keys to the home she'd shared with Duncan for the past fifteen years, tell him to go and hurry up before she made him sorry. She still loved Duncan. He should remember that. She was capable of changing her mind, snatching back his only hope if he hesitated even a moment.

Long before the train arrived, she could hear it coming, the distant rumble getting louder, until it drowned out the river. Her window rattled as it shot past, the thunder receding faster than it had arrived and then, a short eery lull before the river rushed back in.

Over at the pink house, the upstairs light went out. Tomorrow, he might abandon his timetable for the night, perhaps for ever if Duncan gave him a chance. She looked around. In the lamp-light, the bare white walls glowed softly and waited for her.

It wouldn't be much longer now. Tomorrow, she would add a touch of colour, make a start on the future.

Also available from Polygon

Damage Land: *New Scottish Gothic Fiction*
Edited by Alan Bissett
0 7486 6284 7
£9.99

As well as a bloody and turbulent history, Scotland has produced some of the world's most eerie and disturbing fiction. Here the newest and most talented of Scottish writers have plumbed their depths, creating a set of demons for the modern age: Ali Smith's neo-Nazi, Alison Armstrong's transvestite serial-killer, Brian McCabe's abominable neck-boil, James Robertson's mutant mouse, Toni Davidson's confused sado-masochist . . . Be frozen by Helen Lamb's quiet touch or appalled by Andrew Murray Scott's putrescent landscape.

Rattlesnake and Other Tales
Robert Dodds
0 7486 6294 4
£9.99

'Rattlesnake' is the focus of this new collection. More a novella than a short story, it displays Dodds' skills as a gripping storyteller. Set in the expansive desert spaces of Arizona, this is the tale of a woman whose life of abuse at the hands of her husband has led her to murder her tormentor. Horrified by her own life history, she meets a boy whose life seems to mirror her own. As she tries to help him, she slowly, unnoticeably begins to edge towards committing another murder.

Dodds is master of the dark, rich multi-layered story, packing subtle twists and turns into elegantly simple stories.

Polygon
ww.eup.ed.ac.uk

Also available from Polygon

Coloured Lights
Leila Aboulela
0 7486 6298 7
£8.99
Coloured Lights is the first collection of short stories from the winner of the 2000 'African Booker' Caine Prize for African Writing and includes the winning story, 'The Museum'. Surprising and profound, tender and ironic, these beautifully written stories speak of poignant exile and comic social encounters. Aboulela plunges deep to illuminate culture shock and spiritual struggle.

The Burning Mirror
Suhayl Saadi
0 7486 6293 6
£9.99
The Burning Mirror is a mixture of the seamy and the spiritual, the subtle, the baroque and the brutal. The canvas is broad: everything from Glaswegian Asian gangsta stories to themes drawn from various trans-Mediterranean cultures, from the philosophising of a spirit trapped in a bottle to the everyday tribulations of a Catholic Evangelist.

All Polygon titles are available from your local bookshop
or can be ordered direct from our distributors:
Polygon Orders
Scottish Book Source
137 Dundee Street
Edinburgh
EH11 1BG

Polygon
ww.eup.ed.ac.uk